# SHADOWED LOVE

Following a break-up with her partner, Helen Matthews returns to Cornwall to set up a bed and breakfast business in her inherited cottage. There, she meets the arrogant Martin Somerville, who offers to buy her land. Helen refuses, but she faces many more setbacks before she can realise her dream . . . And is it possible that she was wrong about Martin? Could they ever look forward to a future together?

JANET THOMAS

# SHADOWED LOVE

*Complete and Unabridged*

LINFORD
*Leicester*

First published in Great Britain in 2006

First Linford Edition
published 2007

British Library CIP Data

Thomas, Janet
    Shadowed love.—Large print ed.—
Linford romance library
1. Love stories
2. Large type books
I. Title
823.9′2 [F]

ISBN 978–1–84617–760–6

Published by
F. A. Thorpe (Publishing)
Anstey, Leicestershire

Set by Words & Graphics Ltd.
Anstey, Leicestershire
Printed and bound in Great Britain by
T. J. International Ltd., Padstow, Cornwall

This book is printed on acid-free paper

# A New Life

'But, Alex, it's a heaven-sent opportunity!' Helen Matthews looked at his frowning face in disbelief. 'You've been saying for ages that what you'd really like to do is get out of the rat race, start a new life and go and live somewhere peaceful. Haven't you?'

'Yes, I know, but I didn't mean *yet*,' he returned with irritation. He spread his hands wide. 'You know I'm still climbing the ladder at Hobson and Barbary. And I'm pretty sure of stepping up one more rung when old Stephenson retires. He can't last much longer in his state of health.' He glowered down at her and she felt her cheeks flush with disbelief and anger. 'I thought you understood that.'

Helen stepped away from him and walked up and down the room, trying to control her temper.

'But there are loads of estate agents, Alex, all over the place.' She gestured with her hands as she walked, turning to face him again. 'With your qualifications and experience you could get a job anywhere — even if it *is* in deepest Cornwall,' she said pointedly. 'And as Hobson and Barbary are a national firm, it would be perfectly possible to get a transfer if you don't want to leave them.'

'You don't hear what I'm saying, do you?' Alex's voice was rough as he seized her arm and pulled her round to face him.

'I think you're getting carried away with all the excitement.' He gave her arm a shake and went on: 'Yes, your aunt has left you her house and you don't want to sell it. Yes, it's a cottage in Cornwall and yes, it'll be nice to retire to one day, but for goodness' sake — I'm only thirty-three, Helen, and you're what? Twenty-six? Twenty-seven?'

She glared back at him. 'I didn't say *retire*, did I?' she retorted in exasperation. 'Remember we talked about finding somewhere idyllic to live? You could work from home and I could easily find a job locally because there are loads of hotels down there and receptionists are always needed. Then we could laze around in our spare time, enjoying ourselves as if we were on holiday too. Didn't we always say that's what we'd like to do? Or have you forgotten all about that in your great push for *promotion*?' she said through gritted teeth.

'Promotion will only pile on the work and crank up the pressure ... Oh, Alex,' she added in a whisper as her face crumpled, 'what's happening to us? We just don't seem to be on the same wavelength any more.'

The words ended on a sob.

She expected Alex to be ready with a comforting arm, to console, to apologise. To say that of course they would sit down and talk this thing over rationally.

But he did none of those things. Instead he strode to the window, where he came to a halt with his back to her and stood in silence with his arms folded. There was a long pause. Then he slowly turned back into the room and surveyed her across the width of the carpet.

'No,' he said, 'we don't.' His face was like granite. 'But whatever's happening is *your* fault!'

Helen gasped as if she'd been hit, shocked at the harshness of his tone.

'What do you mean — my fault?'

'Ever since you had this grand idea, you've talked and thought about nothing else.'

Helen drew in a shuddering breath.

'Well, *I've* had enough of city life even if you haven't,' she said quietly. She glanced over his shoulder and out of the window at the snarl of traffic and the hurrying crowds below.

It was a bright morning in early summer and in Cornwall, she thought wistfully, the trees would be clothed with new green and the hedgerows dancing with wild flowers . . .

A small voice arose inside her head

and began to torment her. 'Why don't you just go, then?' it whispered. 'You're not dependent on Alex, are you?'

She blinked. No — but we love each other!

The insidious little voice came again. 'And what sort of love is it when neither of you will even consider giving way? You can't even discuss such an important matter without shouting at each other!'

Helen thought deeply for a few moments, then took a ragged breath.

'Well, Alex,' she said steadily as she looked him straight in the face, 'if you really don't want to come with me, I'm quite prepared to go down there by myself. At the end of the month.'

She bit her lip and scuffed at the carpet with her toe, waiting for the storm to break.

To her surprise, however, Alex's voice was positively hearty. 'To sort the place out, you mean? Great idea. I knew you'd see sense when you thought about it. You'll be able to put it in order, then find an agent to put it on the market for you.'

Her heart sank. He hadn't understood what she was getting at. He was relaxed now and all smiles as he walked back towards her. 'No problem.' He made an expansive gesture. 'But make sure you don't work too hard!'

He ran a hand through his flop of blond hair and Helen recognised his engaging grin as the one she'd fallen in love with. She forced herself to ignore it.

'You're not hearing me, Alex,' she responded. 'I mean that I'm going to Cornwall to stay. To live. Permanently.'

She swallowed down a sob and as their eyes locked, she watched the smile fade from his face. Determinedly she ploughed on, ignoring her own misting vision.

'We've been together for so long, Alex, I know that splitting up is going to be like losing a limb, but this is really important to me. I want — I *need* to go home.'

'Splitting up?' His eyebrows rose to his hairline and he seemed to tower over her as he seized her by the shoulders. 'You would seriously go that far just to get your own way?' His face was contorted with rage. 'I never thought you could be so selfish!'

Helen flinched, feeling small and vulnerable as she looked up from her diminutive five foot two into the stormy face above her. But she managed to straighten her shoulders and tilt her chin defiantly.

'Well, if *I'm* being selfish, what does that make you?' she flared at him. 'I thought you wanted a new kind of life as much as I do, but now that the chance has come you've suddenly changed your tune!'

Alex flung away from her with exasperation. 'The time's not right for me, I told you. End of story.' He shoved his hands into his pockets and made for the door. 'Do what you want, then — the way you always do.' Then he strode out of the room and slammed the door behind him.

* * *

'Jane, you said yourself how much you need a holiday. Why don't you come down to Cornwall and stay with me while I sort out Polgarth?'

Jane looked doubtful. 'It sounds lovely and I could do with a break, but Alex might still change his mind and want to come with you — I don't want to play gooseberry.'

'That's not going to happen,' Helen said, her voice quiet but firm. With difficulty, she banished the image of Alex's expression — a mixture of amazement, hurt and fury as he had stormed out of the room that day. But she had stuck to her guns and they were now living in a kind of limbo, only speaking when strictly necessary. Helen's bags were all packed and she was ready to move as soon as she'd worked her notice at work.

She withdrew her plastic cup from the coffee machine and stood back for her friend to take her turn.

'It would be perfect,' she went on as Jane raised an eyebrow. 'We could take sleeping bags and kind of camp out in it while I decide what to do next.'

She wandered over to the window of the staff canteen and gazed out over the city. But rather than the cityscape, in her mind's eye she was seeing the sweeping breakers of the Atlantic rolling in over a tiny Cornish beach, set deep in a rocky valley. Sheer cliffs reared up on either side, pockmarked with man-made tunnels left by the long-ago tin miners, and decaying engine-houses on the cliff tops above still thrust blunt fingers to the sky. Home. She was going home. Like a small wounded animal, she was going back to the nest to try to build a new life for herself — on her own.

Jane joined her and blew inelegantly on her too-hot coffee.

'It's not a bad idea actually. I was

thinking of somewhere abroad — with sun and sea — but I haven't got a lot of leave left this year.' She looked down at Helen from the advantage of her extra height and regarded her thoughtfully. 'And I've never been to Cornwall,' she added.

'It'll be a lot cheaper than abroad — and the sun does shine there, too,' Helen remarked, running a hand through her hair. 'There's plenty of sea as well. You'll love it.'

'How long is it since you actually lived down there?' Jane took a swig of coffee and perched on the corner of the table where they always met for their tea-breaks.

'It must be about ten years. I came up to London to go to business college after I left school, then I stayed on when I got this job.' Helen leaned back in her chair and rested an elbow on its wooden arm as she sipped her coffee. 'A hotel receptionist's salary in Cornwall would never have come anywhere near what I've been getting here.' She tapped her fingers idly against her cup and added with a sigh, 'Then there was Alex, of course.'

'I'm really sorry that things didn't work out for you two,' said Jane with sympathy. 'After you'd been together for so long too.'

Helen crumpled up her empty cup and tossed it into the bin.

'Yes,' she sighed and her shoulders slumped. 'I think perhaps that was part of the trouble — we were getting stale and I hadn't realised it. It took all this business about the cottage to bring things to a head.'

She paused, gazing into space for a moment, then looked back at Jane with a rueful smile. 'And in a strange way I feel relieved, you know? But a bit wobbly as well. I'm a little apprehensive about the future — and sad, too, because I really loved him at first.'

Her eyes were far away. 'I thought he felt the same way, but I can see now that it was only because I was so besotted with him. Looking back, I can see that I was always the one to give in. Every time. I let him have his own way about so many things. And the first time I did dig my heels in — about going back to Cornwall — look what happened!'

A small silence fell. Then she sat up, straightened her shoulders and glanced at her friend.

'So I've decided to make a clean break of it. Throw in the job, go back home and start a new life. I've got some savings, so I'll manage for a while. Will you come with me, Jane?'

The other girl recognised the plea in Helen's eyes and sensed her need for support as she added, 'I'll drive you down and you can come back by train.'

'OK,' Jane replied with a smile. 'I'll come and see this backwater of yours. And it had better be sunny!'

They were both laughing as they headed back to work.

★   ★   ★

It was, too, on the day that they arrived at St Agnes on the north Cornish coast after the six-hour drive down from London.

Helen's cottage stood high up on one slope of the deep wooded valley where the road left the town behind and became a winding lane. Following the course of a small stream, the lane then threaded its way down to the rocky cove half a mile away.

'Helen — it's *fantastic*!' Jane was out of the car and craning her neck over the fence which edged the seaward side of the property. 'Look at that view!' She pointed at the white-fringed, flawlessly blue water. 'Smell the air!' and she took a deep sniff of its tangy freshness, redolent of salt and seaweed. 'You didn't tell me it would be like this!'

Helen laughed at her friend's radiant expression.

'You wouldn't have believed me if I had,' she retorted with a grin as she came to lean on the fence beside her.

But she turned her back on the view to feast her eyes on something even more important, at least to her — her home!

'You lucky thing! How did your family come to live in this place?' Jane asked, still looking all around her, trying to take it all in.

'Oh, my great-grandfather made his money in mining shares. You can still see the relics of the Trevaunance mine up on the cliff-top over there,' Helen pointed, 'and this was their home, his and his family. When they grew up and left, the old couple stayed on and passed it down through the family. My grandparents lived here — he actually worked in the mine — and after them, my aunt. And now it's mine — the cottage and the land. Those two fields behind the house belong to it as well,' she said, pointing. 'I can hardly believe it!'

'So your aunt died a couple of years ago, didn't you say?' Jane enquired.

'Yes,' said Helen. 'She had a long

illness and then went into a nursing home, where she died. The house has been lying here empty since then, waiting for all sorts of legal tangles to be sorted out. I know I could always sell it. In fact, that would be the sensible thing to do, but it's been in the family for so long, I just couldn't bring myself to,' she added as she scrabbled in her bag for the key.

'Come on, I'm dying to get inside. I haven't been back for about six months. Not since — since Alex and I spent our holiday here last September.'

Her stomach gave a flip and she swallowed a lump in her throat as she remembered that wonderful two weeks of cliff-top walks, of sand and surf, and saw again their two golden-tanned bodies stretched out on the beach beneath the summer sun.

But that was all in the past now. Thrusting all thoughts of Alex from her mind, she bent her head to put the key in the lock.

'We'll come back for the luggage in a

minute,' she said and ushered her friend inside.

The interior smelt stuffy and unlived in, and Helen marched from room to room throwing open windows to let the sea breezes sweep through.

'It won't take long to air the place,' she called downstairs to Jane, who was taking a look around the various rooms which opened off the hall.

'This is wonderful,' Jane said as Helen joined her in the kitchen. 'It's a real old country cottage, isn't it?' She looked round at the beamed ceiling, ancient pine dresser and gingham curtains. 'And yet everything's been modernised,' she added as she leaned against the fridge-freezer, 'so you've got the best of both worlds.'

'That's right,' Helen replied. 'I'll show you the upstairs in a minute, but let's get our things in first, shall we?'

They returned to the car and just as Helen was hauling the last of the bags from the boot, she noticed a movement out of the corner of her eye.

She turned to see a young man sauntering down the path towards her. Tanned skin, dark curly hair, firm jaw and an air of jaunty self-confidence — that was Helen's first impression, taking in his crisp blue shirt and chinos, the briefcase tucked under one arm, the engaging grin lighting up his face.

'Hi,' he said as he drew close enough to speak, 'do you know who owns this place? I wanted a word with them.'

'Yes — I do. And you are?' said Helen, tilting her chin to look him in the eye.

The smile faltered and then his face cleared. 'Oh, I see — you're the owner.' He looked her up and down. 'You're obviously busy right now, but could I call round sometime? There's something we need to discuss.'

'Really?' Her brows rose. Tired or not, she would have no peace until she found out what this was about. 'I suppose you'd better come in, Mr — ?'

'Martin Somerville.' He extended a hand and grasped hers. 'My card,' he added, passing it to her.

'Helen Matthews,' she replied absently as she read the wording on his card: *Martin Somerville Ltd., Builder and Estate Agent*. 'And this is my friend, Jane,' she added as the other girl appeared in the doorway.

'Here — let me help with that.'

In a swift movement, the man picked up her bag from beside her feet and followed as Helen led the way indoors.

'Now, Mr Somerville,' she said when they were seated in the bay window of the living-room, overlooking a stunning view of the cove, 'perhaps you can tell me what this is about?'

'Martin — please,' he replied with a smile like that of a mischievous schoolboy.

His grin was very infectious in spite of his cockiness, and Helen couldn't help but return the smile. This man was the sort that could charm the birds from the trees if he put his mind to it, she was thinking.

Just at that moment Jane put her

head around the door.

'Helen, I think I'd better get down to the shop before it closes, and get some essentials. Otherwise we'll have nothing to eat. OK?' She stepped through the doorway and Helen saw that she was clutching an ancient leather shopping bag in one hand. 'This is what reminded me — I found it in the kitchen cupboard,' she said with a giggle. 'It looks about a hundred years old. Perhaps you could enter it for the Antiques Road Show!'

The others joined in her laughter and Helen replied, 'Thanks, Jane. Get whatever you think we need — but get plenty, because this sea air will give us huge appetites.'

As the door banged shut behind Jane, Helen looked expectantly at Martin Somerville.

'It's like this, Helen,' he said, as if they were the best of friends, 'I'm here to do you a favour and make you an offer for that top field of yours.'

He gave another of his engaging grins

as Helen looked blankly back at him. 'My field?' she repeated.

'Yes. I've been looking for a site for some luxury bungalows I intend to build in the area, and that's an ideal position. I've been more or less promised outline planning permission, if I can purchase. Oh, I'll give you a fair price — more than you would get anywhere else, I might add. And since they're good for nothing else but grazing the few goats that are up there now, I'm sure you realise that nobody in their right mind would refuse such an offer.'

Helen could only stare at the dark head as he bent over his papers and carefully extracted one sheet.

'I've got the details here. All you need to do is sign in the couple of places I've marked here ... and here ... ' he indicated. Then, as if he had suddenly noticed the silence in the room, he lifted his eyes enquiringly and met Helen's stormy ones.

'Oh,' he said hastily, 'I hope you

don't think I'm steamrolling you into an instant decision about this, do you? I could call back again tomorrow.'

Helen, who had been thinking exactly that, raised an eyebrow and replied levelly, '*Mr* Somerville — ' She noticed him open his mouth to correct her, but she went on quickly, 'It has obviously not occurred to you that I might not *want* to sell my land.' She held his gaze for a moment.

'As it happens, I already have plans for that field — plans of my own which certainly do not include selling it off to a property developer.'

'Plans? You have? What kind of plans?' His face was a picture of astonishment.

Helen felt like telling him to mind his own business, but faced with the direct stare from those probing eyes, it wasn't easy. Besides, there was nothing secret about it anyway.

'I'm going to set up a bed and breakfast business here,' she replied, 'and once that's up and running I shall expand, and turn the field into a campsite. So you see, I've no intention of selling the land to you or anybody else.'

She gave him a sweet smile and stood up, indicating that their interview was at an end.

'You'll never do it,' came the blunt reply.

Helen gave him a frosty look. 'What did you say?'

He was stuffing papers back into his briefcase and as he snapped the lock shut, he raised his head and met her eyes.

'I said you'll never make it work. St Agnes is too full of holiday lets already. Besides which, there are a lot of very strict planning regulations about that sort of thing, you know.'

'Of course I know,' she replied with her chin in the air. But her heart sank. She knew nothing of the sort — but she would die rather than admit it to this know-all.

Martin Somerville stood up and

picked up his case, clasping it to him as he regarded her with a level stare.

'I hope you do make a go of it,' he said, 'and I wish you the best of luck. But give it twelve months and I think you'll be begging me to take that land off your hands. Well, I can wait,' he said with a nod and turned towards the door.

'Goodbye, Mr Somerville,' Helen said, ushering him out.

'Martin,' he retorted with an impish grin, and Helen laughed in spite of herself as she closed the door behind him.

Well! This was an unexpected start!

She'd hardly had time to think about what he had proposed when the door opened again and Jane came in, laden with carrier bags.

'I just bought what I thought we needed,' she said cheerfully. 'I hope that's OK with you?'

'Anything's OK by me, I'm starving!' Helen replied. 'What have you got that's instant?'

Jane held up a jar of pasta sauce and

a packet of salad leaves.

'Will spaghetti and salad do?'

'Perfect!' Helen said, with a grin. 'I'll set the table.'

'We can bung a couple of potatoes in the microwave, too — and I've got a loaf of crusty bread!'

Twenty minutes later, as they sat over their supper, Helen told her friend all that had passed while she had been out. Jane's eyes widened.

'Well, how about that!' She paused and gave Helen a thoughtful look. 'Actually, all the old biddies in the shop were talking about Martin Somerville. Someone saw him come in here, and you know what villages are like for gossip. So I listened in, and do you know what? You know he said he wants to build up on the back of here?' She twisted a hank of spaghetti expertly round her fork as Helen nodded. 'Well, it seems that he needs your land in order to build an access drive to the new houses.'

Helen stared as Jane added, 'There's

nowhere else for it to go. He's been refused planning permission to take it in from the main road. And without access, of course, his housing development can't go ahead.' Jane shot her friend a meaningful look. 'Now isn't that interesting?'

Helen's fork clattered to the floor as she jumped to her feet and began to pace up and down.

'So *that's* why he was so keen to get me to sell!' she said through gritted teeth. ' 'Take it off my hands' indeed! 'Doing me a favour'!' She turned on her heel. 'The crafty, conniving . . . he never said a word to me about all the rest of it! Oh, if I ever see him again . . . '

Jane chuckled. 'He was quite good-looking, though,' she pointed out mischievously.

'Oh Jane, you're impossible!' Helen scoffed but it was an effort to dismiss the image of the handsome, sunlit, laughing face turned towards her at the open door.

‘Do *you* think it's too risky, what I'm taking on?’ Helen nibbled a thumbnail and her forehead puckered with self-doubt as she finished telling Jane of her plans that evening.

Jane's eyes twinkled. ‘Well, I must admit it takes some imagination to see you as a seaside landlady after being a bright young thing about town for so long!’

‘But I'm not like that inside — not really.’ Helen's face fell. ‘It was only that — that Alex was such fun, at first. We had some great times together . . .’

‘I know,’ said Jane with sympathy.

They were sitting in the bay window sipping their after-dinner coffee, Jane lounging back in her chair with her feet up on a stool, and Helen hunched forward with both hands clasped around her mug, keeping her hands warm as she stared out at the panorama before her.

With her eyes on the swell of the sea

she said, 'Was that hateful man right, do you think? That I'll never make a go of the holiday business?'

'We-ell . . . ' Jane met her friend's anxious eyes as Helen turned back to her. 'I know a fresh start and something completely different is what you need just now, but do think about it very carefully, Helen, won't you?'

Helen nodded as she replied, 'It's not as sudden a decision as it seems, though. I've been turning the idea over in my head ever since this place came to me. In fact, Alex and I talked about it a lot, before he . . . changed his mind.'

'You said an agency has been letting it out already, didn't you?' said Jane, and Helen nodded. 'Which seems to knock on the head the idea that there are too many places offering accommodation, as Martin Somerville claimed. So the big change is that you're taking it over yourself and, of course, that you'll be living on the premises, too. That'll mean one less bedroom for letting.'

Jane paused to admire the setting of the evening sun. The rays were pouring through the window as the enormous fiery ball began to sink below the western horizon.

But Helen's thoughts were still on her house.

'Don't forget the loft conversion, though. There's a big room up there which I thought I might have,' she replied.

The discussion grew more intense as ideas began to flow back and forth between them.

'You know what we should do?' said Jane decisively. 'We should draw up a list of all the things for and against, put them all down on paper, even the small items, and then see how viable the whole thing looks. Don't you think so?'

'Brilliant. I'll fetch some paper and a pen and we'll start right away.'

The sun had long since vanished into the sea and twilight was falling by the time the girls had finished scribbling, but they had produced a long list of 'for' and 'against'.

'Right,' said Helen, stretching her legs which had grown stiff from being curled beneath her. 'I'll read the 'for' list. One — the three bedrooms are already fitted out, one of them with ensuite for which I could charge extra.'

Counting off on her fingers she went on. 'Two — the little boxroom, which is mostly full of junk left from Aunt Grace's day, could be adapted to take bunk beds for two children.

'Three — the dining-room and kitchen could be knocked into one, which would give me a good-sized breakfast room for the visitors and still allow for a partition wall to keep the kitchen private.

'Four — the unbeatable location, a few minutes' walk from the beach, fantastic views, walking, swimming, surfing. There's something for all the family.' She paused to draw breath and looked up expectantly.

'Number four doesn't count,' Jane said sternly. 'That's a natural advantage, not something that you've got any control over. Go on.'

'Right. Well, all this would take very little outlay, the biggest expense being the kitchen conversion. Then, hopefully, with the profits from the first season I could get the camping ground seeded and a shower-toilet block put up for the following year.'

'Fair enough,' Jane said, but her face was solemn as she waved her own list in the air. 'And now for the bad news . . . '

Helen's heart sank but she did her best to look composed as she laid down her pen and paper and sat back to listen.

'One — ' Jane raised a finger. 'This is too big a project for you to handle on your own. You'll have to employ outside help, even if only part-time. Think about it, Helen. There'll be the laundry, the cooking, the shopping, the maintenance, plus all the advertising, bookings and administrative work. You'll never be able to cope with it all.'

Helen nodded. It was a relevant point.

'Then two — there'll be more expenses than you're allowing for. What about insurance? That's a big item. And you haven't allowed for decorating and fitting out the small bedroom either. Plus three — it's August now so you won't be able to open before next season. And with no money coming in you're going to have to live on your savings this coming winter while you're getting the place ready.'

There was a short silence while Helen digested her friend's words. She hated to admit it, but Jane was right — there were just as many 'againsts' as 'fors' for this project. So now she was faced with a decision.

After a moment's silent thought, she said, 'That's a risk I'm willing to take.'

'Helen — '

'No, Jane, listen,' she insisted, tapping absent-mindedly on her chin with her forefinger as she put her thoughts into words, her eyes far away on the darkening sea. 'I've got a fair bit put away in savings. And it's cheaper to live down here anyway. Besides, I could always take out a bank loan to tide me over if I get desperate.'

Jane raised an eyebrow. 'You could, but imagine the state you'd be in if the business failed and you were left with a loan to pay off.'

'Oh, thanks a lot, prophet of doom,' replied Helen with spirit. 'Then I'd get myself a job again, of course,' she added with a slight edge to her voice. 'Working in someone else's hotel, for instance. It's what I do best, remember?'

'Or,' Jane added with a wicked grin, 'I suppose you could always sell off the land to Martin Somerville.'

'Over my dead body!' Helen gave a snort as the image of that treacherous, smiling face surfaced once more.

The next few days were spent alternately relaxing on the beach, for the weather was warm and balmy, and in periods of bustling activity as Helen combined showing Jane around Cornwall with trawling the shops for things she needed for her guest-rooms.

The two friends enjoyed visiting second-hand and antiques shops, hunting for bargains.

'The more I can get out of the way now, the better I can budget for the big things,' Helen said with satisfaction as they arrived home with the car boot filled to the brim once more.

'Thanks for all your help and advice, Jane,' she added with sincerity. 'I would never have got half of this done in the same time on my own.'

'No problem — it's been fun!' her friend replied. 'Come on, let's get this lot inside — I'm dying for a coffee!'

They staggered into the cottage, arms laden with boxes, bags and strange-shaped parcels.

'I can't believe my holiday's nearly over,' Jane went on as they lurched indoors under the weight of all their purchases. 'But it's back to the grind next week.' Her voice was gloomy.

Helen said nothing as a stab of apprehension tightened her nerve endings. This had been no holiday for her, and she wouldn't be going back at the end of it to her old familiar way of life. She was on the threshold of a new and challenging one.

Who could tell what was ahead?

# Another Shock In Store

'I've really enjoyed it, Helen, thanks a million,' Jane said affectionately as they climbed out of the taxi that had brought them to Truro station. Helen's car was in for a much-needed service and was off the road for a few days.

'I'm going to miss having you around,' Helen replied. 'But don't forget to tell anybody who's thinking of a holiday in Cornwall that you can personally recommend the bed and breakfast at St Agnes!'

'I'll do that.' Jane leaned out of the window as the train began to move. 'Best of luck with the project. I'll phone you soon. Bye . . . '

Helen waved her out of sight then turned towards the exit. It was going to be very quiet without Jane's cheerful company, and she felt a stab of something like panic sweep over her at the thought of what lay ahead. Was she doing the right thing or was she burning her comfortable boats for an impossible ideal?

For a moment, part of her wished for a moment that she was on the train heading back to London as well. But only for a moment.

She took a deep breath, straightened her shoulders and walked briskly out of the station. Since the painful break-up with Alex, she was determined to live her life the way she wanted it, free from all the ties that had made her so emotionally vulnerable. Starting from now.

She had tilted her chin so high in her bid for self-confidence that she was taking no heed of where she was putting her feet. Consequently she failed to see the hole in the pavement where a paving-slab had cracked and shifted. She lost her balance and would have fallen flat on her face but for the quick reaction of a young man who was just entering the station. He managed to catch her deftly as her ankle twisted and she pitched forward straight into his open arms.

She gasped and cried out as a searing pain shot through her foot, so sharp that it brought tears to her eyes. Her rescuer steadied her with a hand beneath her elbow as Helen rested her weight on her uninjured foot and stammered her thanks. But when she raised her head, she found herself staring into the eyes of Martin Somerville.

'Oh! It's — it's you.'

'It certainly is,' he nodded. 'How nice to meet you again.'

Helen glowered. Was he poking fun at her?

His face gave nothing away, but his eyes were twinkling as he asked, 'Are you all right?' Looking down at her one-legged stance, he added hastily, 'No, I can see you're not. Your ankle, is it?' His face was full of concern now.

'It'll be all right in a minute. I twisted it a bit, that's all.' She bit her lip as she put her foot to the ground and tested it. 'It's thanks to you it wasn't worse,' she replied in all fairness. She busied herself with her belongings, straightened her jacket and ran a hand through her hair, all to give herself something to do while she regained her composure.

'I just happened to be in the right place at the right time,' he replied. 'I only came in to buy a paper, then wow, lucky me — there was a pretty girl just waiting to throw herself into my arms.'

He grinned widely and Helen scowled. Of all the people in Truro why did it have to be *him*?

'That'll teach me to look where I'm going, won't it?' She forced herself to smile politely at him. 'Thanks again anyway. I must go. Goodbye.' She took a few painful steps but couldn't help limping. She could feel his eyes on her back, watching her.

He took a couple of strides to catch up with her and grasped her arm.

'Let's go and have a coffee in the buffet here and you can rest that ankle.

Walking on it will only make it worse. Then I'll give you a lift back.'

There was nothing Helen would have liked more at that moment, and she knew that he was perfectly right. But there was no way she was going to put herself under any obligation to this man, and wild horses wouldn't have dragged her to the coffee-shop with him. So she gathered the remains of her bruised dignity and pasted a smile on her face.

'Thanks, but no thanks. I have an appointment actually,' she said with a glance at her watch, 'and my foot will be fine now. Bye.'

She could tell that he was watching her again, his eyes boring into her back as she made her way down the hill towards the town, but she resisted the temptation to look back at him.

With iron willpower she managed to walk the whole way, hardly limping at all. However she turned down the first side-street she came to, desperate to remove herself from his line of vision.

Heaving a deep, shuddering sigh of relief, she slowed her pace and allowed herself to limp unseen.

Arriving at a small and fairly quiet square, she sank thankfully on to a bench at a bus stop.

Deep in her own thoughts, she gradually became unaware of the red Cavalier rounding the corner and slowing as it drew level until the driver tooted his horn.

She looked up. An arm raised in greeting, white teeth flashed in a broad smile. She groaned. For the second time in half an hour he had caught her — literally — wrong-footed. Her feeble cover had been blown and she had been made to feel a fool again. Here was the bus, and now he would see her getting on to it . . .

★　★　★

'Morning, my 'andsome. Your friend gone back now, have she?' Helen had been tidying up the small front garden, where a few tubs of hardy geraniums stood beneath the window and some tamarisk bushes waved their feathery branches in one corner. The tubs were full of weeds, and a clump of nettles had rooted itself in between the shrubs.

She glanced at the backs of the row of three cottages which stood farther down the steep slope. They were low enough for her to have an uninterrupted view right over their roofs to the sea, but sufficiently close to carry on a conversation with the woman who had called to her from one of the gardens as she hung out her washing.

'Hello, Ruth,' Helen called back and strolled to the dividing fence. 'Yes, Jane went home a few days ago. She had to get back to work.'

'Nice young lady.' Ruth picked up a shirt from the basket at her feet and shook it out before pegging it on the line. 'I met her in the shop the other day, just when you got here. We had a bit of a chat.'

Helen smiled as she recalled Jane

laughing about the gossiping old village biddies.

Ruth Taylor hung up a couple of towels beside the shirt and they began to flap wildly in the stiff onshore breeze.

'Talking about that Mr Somerville, we was.'

Helen's stomach lurched but she replied in what she hoped was an off-hand manner. 'Oh, yes? What about him?'

'Man must be made of money, I said. What with all these houses he's going to build up on top of the hill, and this here luxury bungalow what he's putting up for himself too.'

She pointed a finger in the direction of property over the hedge from Polgarth. As Helen followed her gaze, she became aware of a cement mixer turning and she could see a couple of men in hard hats coming out of the gate, one holding a clipboard in his hand as they turned to look back at the site.

'Looks like you're going to be

neighbours soon, don't it?' said Ruth with a smile.

'*What?*' Helen's pretence at nonchalance vanished. She gaped openmouthed at her neighbour. 'You mean that — that house belongs to Martin Somerville, and he's going to *live* there?'

Obviously pleased to have made such an impact with her snippet of news, Ruth Taylor nodded solemnly. 'Oh, yes. He's knocked down the old place and cleared the site so he can build all new, see.'

She bent to her washing basket again, then, as she straightened up, went on: 'They do say how he made a lot of money on the stock market in London and then he come down here when he'd had enough of city life.'

A colourful tablecloth was now fluttering on the line beside the towels.

'Decided to settle here like, and go into the building trade. He haven't been here more than a few months. He rented a house up the road,' she

43

pointed a finger. 'It do belong to my cousin, Henry, that's how I knows.'

Helen was fuming. To have that man practically on her doorstep, to be bumping into him whenever she went in or out — how could she stand it? But, she realised, she would just have to put up with it because there was no way she was going to change her own plans.

She glanced towards the building site again and stood on tiptoe to peer through a gap in the hedge. The builders were only at the foundation stage, so it would obviously be some time before it was ready for occupation.

Hopefully by then her own business would be under way and they would both be kept too busy to see much of each other.

'I heard you was going into the holiday trade — that true, is it?' Ruth Taylor asked and Helen gasped in amazement. How the jungle telegraph had discovered that already, she had no idea — unless Jane had mentioned it. 'I hope you know what you're doing, my 'andsome. A very chancy business, that is.' Ruth sniffed and ran a hand over her iron-grey perm.

'So people tell me,' Helen replied with a slight edge to her voice. It would be nice to get some encouragement from someone sometime.

She pulled up a few weeds from underneath the bushes as her neighbour went on chatting.

'You'll be wanting a builder yourself, shouldn't wonder, for your alterations and suchlike, will you?'

Helen raised her head with sudden interest. 'I shall, as soon as I get planning permission through. Why? Do you know someone reliable, Ruth — someone you could recommend?'

Her neighbour nodded, folded her arms over her ample bosom and took a step nearer. 'I do know just the man you want, my 'andsome.'

'Oh, that's great! You see, I've no idea who to ask and there are such a lot of dodgy firms around . . . ' Helen lowered her voice and glanced behind her although there was no way that the men next door could have heard.

'Yes. Jack Roskilly's my brother-in-law,' Ruth replied, lowering her own voice and nodding with an air of conspiracy. 'Some good worker he is and everyone round here will tell you so. Want me to mention it to him, do you?'

'Oh, yes, please. Ask him to call round for a chat. I'll need some advice on a few things to begin with.'

'All right, my 'andsome, I'll tell him.' Ruth eyed Helen with open curiosity. 'Where are you from, maid? You do sound as if you're Cornish. Come from round here, do you?'

'Not far away,' Helen replied, tugging at a dandelion. 'My mother lives in Truro. She's a widow. But I've been working in London for ten years, ever since I left school.'

'I see.' Having found out what she wanted to know, and seeing from Helen's bent head that no more interesting information was to be

46

forthcoming, Ruth turned to go. 'Well, I can't stand here chatting all day. Must get on. These clothes won't peg themselves on the line.'

Helen smiled at the implication that she was interrupting a busy woman and went indoors to clean herself up, having done enough gardening for one day.

She made herself a coffee and had just flopped into a chair to relax, trying not to think about Martin Somerville and his plans, when there came a ring at the front door.

She went to answer it with the mug still in her hand and there he was on the doorstep, precisely as if she had conjured him up out of thin air.

His eyes fixed on the coffee mug. 'I'd love one, thanks.'

Lost for words. Helen stepped back and somehow he was in the hall and she was closing the door behind him. How had that happened? She'd had no intention of inviting him in, but he'd already made his way down to the kitchen and before she knew it, she was making another cup of coffee.

'I was passing, so I thought I'd just call in to see if your ankle's better.' He perched on a corner of the pine table and sipped his drink, his quizzical eyes meeting hers over the rim of the mug.

'Oh, yes, it's perfectly all right now, thanks.'

She was seething, both at the aplomb with which he'd installed himself and her own feebleness at letting him do so. Consequently, her next remark came out in a rush and sounded more aggressive than she actually meant it to.

'Why didn't you tell me that you need my land for access to your site?'

He regarded her calmly. 'I didn't know I had to,' he replied with some sarcasm and perfect truth. 'I'm prepared to offer you a fair price, as I said. Should I have asked for your permission as well?'

'Of course not. I didn't mean it like that. But it was a . . . surprise, that's all.' Her voice tailed off as she took a mouthful of coffee. Surprise? Shock would be nearer the mark. It was as if he hadn't been totally honest with her. But how could she explain rationally how let-down she felt?

Besides that, he had to be the most arrogant man she had ever met, she thought. Having strolled uninvited into her house, he now seemed perfectly at home there, nonchalantly swinging one leg and looking appraisingly around the room. She noticed that he was wearing designer jeans and an expensive-looking cashmere sweater which spoke of money allied with good taste.

'It was another surprise to find out that you're building a house for yourself next door to me.' Helen glared at him, knowing she was sounding waspish, but not caring. 'Don't you think it would have been common courtesy to just mention it in passing?'

'Well, now.' He drained his mug and slid from the table in one easy movement. 'Since you seem to have found out all you want to know pretty accurately over the grapevine, courtesy seems hardly necessary in the circumstances.'

He rinsed the mug at the sink, left it upside down to drain and turned to face her with a grin, having neatly placed her in the wrong once again.

Fuming, Helen tried to think of a smart rejoinder but failed.

'Nice little place you've got here,' Martin remarked, strolling around with his hands in his pockets. 'How many bedrooms are there?'

Helen was dying to tell him to mind his own business, but it was impossible to put this man down. So she glared at him and replied, 'Three, plus my own room in the loft.'

She placed her own mug in the sink then strolled towards the door, hoping that he would take the hint.

\*   \*   \*

To her surprise he did, but he paused as he passed the window, his eyes caught by the assortment of odds and ends

Helen had dumped on the sill. When she'd been turning out the boxroom, which was full of stuff that Aunt Grace had hoarded over the years, she'd come across a shoebox full of bits and pieces which she had brought downstairs and tipped out onto the wide windowsill while she sorted through it.

Broken spectacles, pieces of string and several rusty nails were part of it, but she had also come across a quaint little statuette. The figure was that of a seated woman with a cat's head. It was an unusual object which had somehow appealed to her and she had placed it on the window-sill as an ornament.

Martin carefully lifted it up for a closer look. He peered intently at it for a moment, then held it up to the light from the window.

'Well, well,' he said, meeting her frosty stare as she seethed once more at his cheek. 'Have you any idea what this is?' His face was alight with genuine interest.

'I haven't finished sorting through

that stuff yet.' Her oblique reply was a face-saving exercise for she had taken it at face value for what it seemed — a statuette of a woman's figure but having the head of a cat. She had no intention of admitting to him that she had had no idea it might be anything special.

Martin dusted off the object against his sleeve. Made from smooth black stone, its ears were longer and more pointed than that of an ordinary domestic cat, while its yellow eyes were amazingly realistic.

'Was your aunt ever in Egypt?' he asked with a quick glance up at her.

'I don't know,' she replied, then, thinking how feeble this sounded, she added, 'She was my great-aunt, and I never really knew her. She came from my father's side of the family and we rather lost touch after he died. I've spent such a lot of time away from Cornwall as well.'

Martin nodded. 'I just wondered because this, you see — and I think it's genuine — is a figure of the cat-goddess they called Bast.' He was turning it over in his hand. 'Cats were sacred animals in ancient Egypt. They were mummified after death, just like important people.'

She was thinking what an unlikely person he was to be interested in such a subject when he, as if he had been reading her mind, remarked: 'I've been fascinated by Egyptian culture ever since I went to the Tutankhamun exhibition in Dorset when I was a child. Did you ever see it?'

Helen shook her head. 'No. Dorset, did you say? I thought it happened in London *years* ago.'

Martin smiled. 'That was the original one — with the real artefacts. No, this is a permanent exhibition made up of exact replicas of the treasures. It's laid out just like the actual tomb was when Howard Carter discovered it. Our school went on a trip to see it soon after it opened in nineteen seventy-two. I was ten years old then and living in Shaftesbury.'

'Is that where you come from
— Dorset?' So he's four years older
than me, Helen was thinking, and
wondered why it should matter.

'Yes. I studied Fine Arts at college
and then went into the auction
business. I've always loved antiques and
the history behind them. I worked at
Christie's for a while. Then I moved
into real estate.'

Helen nodded, suddenly interested in
the other side of this surprising man.

'That exhibition was fantastic and
fired me up with a love of Ancient
Egypt which has never worn off. I've
always promised myself I'd go to the
Valley of the Kings one day, see the
pyramids, cruise down the Nile . . .'

His expression was dreamy and
Helen caught another glimpse of the
real person behind the image of
the high-handed businessman. And,
she thought idly, how much more
pleasant this one was . . .

'This would have been placed in
someone's home as a guardian against

evil,' Martin went on. 'It's beautifully made. Feel how smoothly it's been polished.'

He stroked the object with a finger and for a split second as Helen bent forward to take a closer look, his springy hair brushed against her cheek. She jumped and recoiled as if a snake had bitten her, then felt foolish in case he'd noticed.

'I read an account somewhere of a chap who killed a cat in ancient Egypt, and he was set upon by a furious mob and lynched,' Martin told her. 'And when a domestic cat died, the family went into mourning and its body was preserved with great ceremony.'

'No good expecting these goddesses to stoop so low as to catch rats and mice then,' Helen replied with a chuckle. 'I suppose they sat on fine cushions and were fed by hand on the finest fish the Nile could provide!'

She could hear herself babbling in order to cover her confusion and was relieved when Martin good-naturedly joined in her laughter.

He put the cat back on the sill and said, 'Take good care of that. It's probably worth something as an antique.'

'Oh, I won't be selling it,' Helen replied. 'I shall keep it as an heirloom — and I'd like to try to find out more about Aunt Grace's life. I really should do if I'm going to live in her house.'

'Well, thanks for the coffee,' said Martin, moving again towards the door. 'You'll be kept pretty busy this winter getting your business under way, I suppose.'

'I certainly shall,' Helen replied.

'Well, you'll need a builder soon, of course — but you do have my card, don't you?' He gave her a radiant smile. 'My firm is very reasonable. Just get in touch when you're ready.'

There it was again — the cheek of the man! Surely he was joking — wasn't he? Helen was bursting to know for sure, but she managed to lift her chin and reply levelly, 'Thank you all the same, but I've already had a builder recommended to me.'

'You have? Who?' His brows drew together sharply. 'Not some local cowboy handyman type, I hope?'

But Helen had had enough. 'I'm afraid that's none of your business,' she said sweetly, ignoring the dark eyes boring into hers. 'And now you must excuse me. As you remarked, I'm a pretty busy person.'

He was still glaring as she ushered him out and he strode down the path without another word.

Helen closed the door behind him with hands that shook, hating herself for getting so steamed up — but there was something about him that rubbed her up the wrong way every time they met! And yet, when there was no friction between them, he could be so nice . . .

# Fingers Crossed!

Having been back in Cornwall for over a month, Helen could no longer ignore the fact that she had yet to go and see her mother. Since Jane's visit, which had lasted a fortnight, she'd been so busy getting to know the house and what was in it, and working out her long-term plans, that the time had absolutely flown.

A meeting with her mother wasn't something she was looking forward to; they were as different as chalk and cheese and had never been close. But it was almost a year since she'd seen her, so she could hardly *not* go. Phone calls were all very well but Helen knew where her duty lay and would rather go of her own accord than wait to be summoned.

'Lovely to see you, dear.' Laura Matthews kissed the air somewhere around her daughter's cheek and ushered her into the bungalow amidst a cloud of expensive perfume.

Impeccably made up with not a hair out of place, Laura always made Helen feel like a street urchin. She glanced ruefully down at her jeans and casual shirt as she replied, 'Hello, Mum, how are you?'

She followed the older woman into the sitting-room which overlooked the tidal reaches of the River Fal and took a seat in the bay window. Laura sank down into a velvet-covered armchair beside her and patted her hair.

'Oh, not too bad. Rushed off my feet as usual. There's the W.I. monthly meeting coming up and I have to bake for that. The Friends of the Hospital are having a fundraising bazaar and I'm doing a stall for them. Then there's the Oxfam shop — I still work there two mornings a week . . . '

Nothing changes, Helen thought. Laura was the archetypal committee woman and charity worker and revelled in it, although she never ceased to complain about the amount of time it entailed.

As she listened, a polite smile fixed on her face, Helen felt a sudden flash of insight. It hadn't occurred to her before but it was suddenly clear that all this frantic activity was designed to fill her mother's otherwise empty life and that she was actually more dependent on the charitable causes than they were upon her. It was a little saddening and for the first time, she felt a glimmer of sympathy for her mother.

At last, Laura's catalogue of her responsibilities had run its course and she was saying, 'Well now, tell me all *your* news. You're still determined to go through with this bed and breakfast thing, I suppose?'

'I certainly am.' Helen nodded with enthusiasm. 'It'll be really exciting, running my own business. I've already arranged to have some alterations done to the house, and I'll be getting the planning application for the camp-site in shortly.'

'Exciting maybe — and risky, I'm sure,' Laura replied, and Helen groaned inwardly. Not another one!

'I was really disappointed to hear that you'd broken up with Alex.' Laura gave her daughter a disapproving look. 'He sounded a very sensible young man — just the sort you need.'

Helen pulled a face. 'It takes two people to make a relationship work, Mum,' she said quietly. 'This one had run its course.'

'Hmm.' Laura pursed lips disapprovingly and drummed her fingers on the arm of her chair. 'Well, I'll go and make us a cup of tea.'

Helen followed her into the tiny, spotless kitchen. When she had been a child, before her father had died of a heart attack when she was ten years old, they had lived in the country in an old converted barn which she had loved. The kitchen then had been the hub of the house, with a warm and welcoming Aga at its heart — a complete contrast to this neat but somehow uninviting room.

She recalled with a rush of nostalgia how she and her younger brother had spent every day of every school holiday roaming the fields and woods. This had instilled in them both a great love of the outdoors which had remained with them ever since.

Torn between this love and the practicality of earning a living as she had grown older, Helen had taken her mother's advice and gone in for secretarial work. During a restless period when she had hankered for a life somewhere more lively than in a Cornish market town, she'd gone up to London and enrolled in a business college, which was what had led to the position in the hotel where she'd first met Alex.

'I'm really glad to be back in Cornwall, Mum,' she said with feeling as she leaned on the window-sill and glanced out at the sparkling river. 'I'd had enough of city life. It gave me a good living at the time, but I sometimes used to feel that I couldn't breathe properly. I really missed the sea breezes.'

'And what are you going to live on until this business of yours is up and running?' Laura enquired, setting a tray with an embroidered cloth and putting out dainty cups and saucers. Helen thought of the cheap and cheerful mugs which were all she ever used herself, and smiled.

'Oh, I've got enough saved to tide me over,' she replied airily and changed the subject, unwilling to give her mother an opportunity to pour cold water on any of her ideas.

\* \* \*

Back in the sitting-room, she sipped her tea and reached for a home-made cookie. 'Have you heard from Tim lately?' she asked. 'I haven't spoken to him for a while.'

Her mother crossed elegant legs and placed her cup and saucer on the low table between them.

'Not for a couple of months, but you know what he's like. If he's not mapping out the haunts of the lesser-spotted doodlebug or some other obscure creature, he's got his head buried in books about it!'

Helen laughed at this accurate description of her academic brother, who worked for the local Nature Trust and was heavily involved in all things ecological.

'I keep telling him that it's high time he found himself a nice girl and settled down, but it's like water off a duck's back,' Laura complained.

'Or a doodlebug's,' Helen replied with a grin and they shared a rare moment of empathy.

Making the most of this cosy moment, Helen went on thoughtfully, 'Mum, how much do you know about Aunt Grace's early life? Before she settled in St. Agnes, I mean?'

'Grace?' Laura raised finely-pencilled brows. 'Well, she was a school-teacher, as you know. She taught geography all her working life and travelled a lot — especially after she retired, I believe. That's when she settled in St. Agnes, of course.'

'Did she ever go to Egypt, do you know?'

'Egypt? Oh yes. She was potty about all things Egyptian — a bit eccentric with it, actually. She used to go out there most summers and get herself involved in archaeological digs if she could. When she went into the residential home she gave the museum masses of curios and artefacts that she had collected over the years.'

There was a pause as Laura took another dainty sip of tea from her cup.

'She used to write to your father regularly when he was a boy,' she went on. 'I think she was quite fond of him in a distant kind of way. Grace never married or had children of her own, of course.'

She paused, trying to recall what she knew.

'I know she was in Egypt in nineteen twenty-two, the same year that Tutankhamun's tomb was discovered, because your father had some photos which she'd sent him.'

'Have you still got them?' Helen asked with interest.

'The photos or the letters?' Laura enquired.

'Well, both really.'

'Yes, I have actually. I saved them for you when you were a child, but you never showed much interest. You were such a hoyden — always running wild outdoors. I used to despair of you sometimes, as a daughter.'

Helen felt a twinge of guilt. With maturity she could see why she and her mother had never been close. Laura had wanted a 'girly' girl and instead had been landed with a tomboy. But that was hardly Helen's fault, was it?

'I'd love to see anything you've got,' she replied, deciding to ignore Laura's other remarks. 'I've been thinking about her a lot since I moved into the cottage.

It would be nice to know a bit more about her.'

'I'll see what I can find,' her mother promised as Helen rose to make her farewells.

Helen breathed a sigh of relief once she was safely ensconced in her car once more and on her way home, duty done.

★   ★   ★

Jack Roskilly the builder turned up one morning in a battered old truck which had seen better days, and rattled up Helen's drive in a cloud of exhaust fumes. Big, burly and balding, he had penetrating blue eyes, and an engaging grin which showed two missing teeth.

'So you see,' said Helen as she showed him into the kitchen, 'I need this dividing wall knocked down to make these two rooms into one. That should be quite simple to do, don't you think?'

'Hmm.'

The man tapped at the wall, put an ear to it, tapped again in a different spot, then sucked in air between his teeth and let it out in a sigh.

His face was grave as he finally turned to her and said, 'Well now, I wouldn't be so sure about that, my handsome.'

Helen's heart sank. 'Whyever not?' she said in surprise. 'Is there a problem?'

'You could say so. Because this here is a supporting wall, that's why.' He slapped it with one hand. 'The kitchen was put on as an extension after the house was built, see, and they used the original outside wall to rack it on to.' He looked at her worried face and went on, 'Oh, it can be done all right, but 'twill mean putting a girder in to take the strain, see.'

'And that will be a big job — and expensive,' Helen finished for him.

'I'm afraid so, my handsome. No good saying otherwise. But I got a few contacts in the trade and I'll do it for the best price I can.' Jack paused and looked around. 'What else did you want doing, then?'

'That's the biggest job,' Helen replied. 'But I'd like you to look at the small boxroom as well.' She moved towards the stairs. 'It's been closed up for so long that the damp has got in and some of the plaster has fallen off the walls. There, you see?' She opened the door and pointed.

The builder squeezed in between the stacked pieces of furniture and, whistling tunelessly under his breath, tapped around with the handle of a trowel which he produced from a pocket in his overalls. Several lumps of plaster tumbled to the floor and Helen winced.

To her relief, though, he turned to her with a grin and said, 'No problem there. That wall's sound enough. The whole room do want re-plastering, but that's all.' He nodded and eased his way out. 'That the lot, is it?'

'There'll be decorating, of course, but yes, I think so,' Helen replied. 'I'm worried about that kitchen wall though. Can you work out an estimate, Jack, and let me have it as soon as possible?' She led the way downstairs. 'I can't make any decisions, you see, until I know what it's going to cost.'

'Course I can, my 'andsome. Drop it round to you in a day or two, I will.'

'Thank you.'

'Bye now, Miss.'

Helen closed the door behind the builder and leant back against it as she absorbed the implications of the headache he had landed her with.

Now she was in a quandary — whether to go ahead and treat the extra expense as an investment, or to play safe and leave the rooms as they were.

She wandered outside and took the steeply sloping path towards the beach. She needed to think and could always do that better in the open air.

It was now the end of August and the cove was full of families enjoying the perfect weather. She strolled across the sand and, leaving the crowds behind, clambered around the headland by way of the rocky foreshore to a further small cove which was less populated.

Here she perched on an outcrop above the sea, wrapped her arms around her knees, and rested her chin upon them as she gazed out to sea.

The tide was coming in and beginning to suck and slap at the rocks below. The sea was a fantastic shade of turquoise around the rocks, and a pure azure blue farther out, shading to amethyst and indigo beneath the shadow of the passing clouds. Helen thought of the life she had left behind in London and could truthfully say she regretted nothing.

'Not even Alex?' asked a small voice inside her as an image of his familiar face surfaced in her mind.

She sighed, feeling suddenly very alone. It would have been nice to have someone to talk to and to share her problems with. But no, Alex was part of the past now and she had more pressing things to occupy her time.

After a while, she stretched and got to her feet. Heading for home, she realised that the beautiful view and the atmosphere of the sea had worked its magic on her as it always did. She was feeling more relaxed about the whole thing.

Sadly, the underlying problem was still unsolved.

★ ★ ★

She spent several restless nights in spite of telling herself to wait and see what the bill was going to be before worrying about it. When the estimate did arrive, it was actually less than her fearful imaginings had made it out to be, though it was still large enough to be a headache.

But then one day she awoke with her head as clear as the patch of morning sky she could see through her window. She knew without doubt what her decision would be. Of course she would have the work on the kitchen done. It was essential if she were to set up in the bed and breakfast business, for as things stood at the moment there was no way the room was big enough to serve breakfast in. Simple. So why had she been dithering for so long?

She picked up the phone and called Jack Roskilly right away before she could have second thoughts.

'I'll be round next Monday, my 'andsome,' came the cheery reply.

As good as his word, the builder and his son moved in on Monday morning and half an hour later had reduced the house to a shambles, thick with flying dust and loud with the sound of hammers and falling blocks. Helen fled outside for air and went for a walk along the cliffs, drinking in the view while she waited for things to subside indoors.

Taking the track which wound to the left above the beach, she followed it as it threaded its way through outcrops of granite rock golden with lichen. Beyond these was a breathtaking sheer drop to the sea a hundred feet or more below. The cliffs were awash with mounds of brilliant pink thrift and white bladder campion, while swags of butter yellow kidney vetch tumbled over the edge and streamed down towards the sea which roared and boomed in the caverns beneath.

Some of the caverns were man-made, she knew, for evidence of the former extensive mine workings were all around. An old engine-house and several chimneys reared on the skyline and there were abandoned shafts and the crumbling walls of derelict buildings everywhere. Dotted about between the shore-line and where she was standing she could see several adits, apertures which had been cut in the cliff-face to drain water out of the mines or to let fresh air in.

Helen perched on a rocky outcrop and looked over, imagining the scene in mid-winter when the screaming gales from the Atlantic would whip up the water into a frenzy and both would hurl themselves relentlessly at this forbidding spot, and she paused to marvel at the toughness and courage of the men who had worked in these exposed conditions all their lives.

At last she glanced at her watch and headed back to the house.

She was climbing slowly up the steep lane which led from the beach and was approaching the house when she became aware of voices coming from Martin Somerville's partly-built bungalow. Unable to restrain her curiosity, she glanced over the hedge to see a tall, elegant woman with a small child in her arms coming down the path chatting to one of the builders and holding another child by the hand.

As they reached the gap where a gate would one day be, Helen overheard the man say, 'Ok, Mrs Somerville, we'll get that seen to for you, no problem. I'll give you a ring when we've finished and you can come and have another look.'

Faced with this evidence of Martin's

wife and family, Helen wondered, as her heart took a sudden dive, why he had never mentioned them in conversation. Yet why should he have done?

She turned her back on the little family group as they climbed into a car parked in the lane and returned to the chaos indoors.

★  ★  ★

Jack Roskilly proved to be a skilful and reliable workman, but he was a Cornishman and consequently could not be hurried. 'We'll do it dreckly, my 'andsome, don't you fret,' was his stock answer to all her anxious questions, and if she heard this once, she heard it a dozen times as she chewed her fingernails in frustration.

In vain she tried to impress upon him the need for urgency — that the business had to be up and running by Easter at the latest, which was when the holiday season began. It was such a short season anyway, she knew that if she wasn't ready by then she would never have a chance to recoup her outlay in the few months that were left.

'Don't you worry, maid,' came the inevitable and unfazed reply. 'Nothing good wasn't never done in no hurry. Can't plaster these walls till they've dried out proper. So we'll see you again end of next week.'

The conversation was typical of many which left Helen tearing her hair in frustration during the winter months. Wild horses would never have made her admit it, but it crossed her mind to wonder more than once, as she glanced out of the window at the rapidly rising walls of his bungalow, whether she should have taken on Martin Somerville's construction firm after all. But hers was a different sort of job, of course, and anyway, it was too late now.

The kitchen was looking as if a bomb had hit it. There was a permanent layer of gritty dust underfoot which persisted no matter how often she cleaned it up, and which coated the soles of her shoes and spread inevitably to all the other rooms as she went to and fro. Every item of furniture that had not been swathed in dust sheets was covered with a grey film of grime, and even the bath-water had a gritty feel about it and a faint layer of scum on top.

She felt like screaming. Even the weather seemed to have turned against her as a spell of the moist, mild drizzle for which Cornwall is renowned, drifted in and seemed set to remain.

After a week of it and little sign of the plaster drying out, Helen leaned her elbows on the window-sill and peered out into the gloom, sunk to an all-time low. She hadn't been as downcast as this since her break-up with Alex. And the knowledge that she was too far into the scheme to abandon it now — too much of her money was already sunk in cement and concrete blocks for that — did nothing to cheer her up.

To take her mind off the gloom, she went upstairs and switched on the second-hand computer which she had bought soon after arriving at the cottage, when it had seemed a good idea to advertise the business over the Internet. She had read somewhere that effective promotion was the surest way of selling a product, and while Jane had been staying with her, the two of them had spent quite a few evenings designing a website for her business.

Now, with more confidence than she felt at the moment, Helen fed in all the details of the letting and crossed her fingers that everything would actually be ready in time.

Well, she thought when she'd finished, there's nothing I can do now but wait.

So saying, she temporarily abandoned everything and went to spend Christmas with her mother and Tim.

# A Shoulder To Cry On

'So, how are things with the Trust, Tim?' Helen enquired of her brother as they lounged, sated with food and drink, in Laura's comfortable deep armchairs. Their mother had gone to call on an elderly friend next door and they were temporarily alone in the house.

'And what project are you working on now? It seems ages since we've had a proper chat,' she commented.

'It *is* ages. You know how I hate the phone for chatting. It's just not the same.' He ran a hand through his shock of thick fair hair and grinned at her. 'I've been meaning to come over and see your place for ages, but I've been so busy lately that the time just hasn't been there. But I will — soon.'

'Great,' Helen replied. 'I'll look forward to it. Better give me a ring first to make sure I'm in.'

Tim uncrossed his long legs and rose to his feet. 'Let's go out for a walk — I need exercise after that huge lunch and it'll do you good too.'

'I know that makes sense,' said Helen, 'but I'm really comfortable at the moment.' Then she glanced at him and saw the determined look in his eyes. 'Oh, all right then,' she replied with a sigh, 'but only a short one, mind — not one of your muddy hikes.'

'Would a sedate stroll along by the river suit your ladyship?' His blue eyes twinkled as he held out an arm and Helen took it with a giggle. They had always got on well, although she was four years older than Tim.

As they wandered along beneath the leafless trees and watched the waterfowl on the mud-flats of the tidal river, Tim said with a smile, 'You asked me what I'm working on now. Well — you're going to find this hard to credit because it sounds like science fiction, but I'm not pulling your leg, honestly. Someone in our department has discovered a very rare fern.' He paused for effect and grinned at his sister's blank expression.

'A *fern*?' she said scornfully. 'Is that it — a fern?'

'No, that's not 'it' by any means.' Tim's face was serious now. 'It's something special — a detoxifying fern. That's why I've been so busy. Let me explain,' and the tone of his voice changed to the tone which Helen recognised as the one he used for his lectures

'This is *Pteris cretica*, Cretan fern, which is able to detoxify soils poisoned by arsenic.' Tim stopped and turned to her, his face aglow with enthusiasm.

'Think about what that means, Helen — *arsenic*. The most widespread soil contaminant in Cornwall. Found in most of the old mining areas which are so poisoned by it that nothing will grow there and where the land is left useless and derelict.'

'I see.' Helen's quick brain was now racing ahead. 'So if this fern can be cultivated it would clean up the land so that it could be brought back into use again. Is that the idea?'

'It certainly is. And because of our mild climate, the fern could be developed here. Think about what that would mean.' His eyes were shining. 'Cornwall could be at the forefront of a low-cost method of soil treatment which other places might be interested in as well. That can't be bad, can it? It would be good for jobs and good for the county too.

'But you see what I meant?' he said, looking down into her face with a broad grin on his own. 'That it sounds like something out of science fiction?'

Helen giggled. 'I'm just trying to imagine it,' she said. 'This little plant creeping around on the old mine dumps, chomping away and saying to itself, 'Wow, arsenic! Goody, goody, give me more — yum, yum!'

'Idiot!' he chuckled and gave her a dig in the ribs. 'Sometimes I despair of you, I really do. We'd better get you home again before the men in white coats come to lock you up!'

And arm in arm they both turned, laughing, to head back upriver.

★　★　★

The break had done Helen good and she was feeling more upbeat by the time she returned home to Polgarth. Also the weather had improved, the mist and drizzle having given way to clear skies and a crisp north-westerly wind which was cold but exhilarating. Huge waves were pounding into the bay now and crashing spectacularly against the cliffs in clouds of billowing spray.

She grinned as she took a gust of salty air full in her face and sniffed appreciatively while she dug in her pocket for the house key.

Lying on the doormat was a pile of mail. Helen snatched it up eagerly and tore open the envelopes — and found half a dozen summer bookings! She swallowed hard, her heart thumping wildly. Now she really was committed.

The pressure to have everything ready in time had taken on a new dimension.

She looked apprehensively around the kitchen, picturing what had still to be done. But the change in the weather had been drying out the plaster while she was away and it was looking very much better.

Her spirits rose a little. Tomorrow Jack and his son would be back to continue with the work and she would ask one of them to tackle the boxroom. Then, when that was done, she would decorate the room herself. It would save time and she was looking forward to transforming it into an attractive bedroom.

⋆　⋆　⋆

'How's it all going then, Helen?' It was a few days later and she was out in the garden hanging up some washing on the rotary line round at the side of the house.

At the unexpected voice she jumped

and whirled around to see Martin Somerville in a hard hat, jeans and work-boots looking over the hedge that separated their properties.

She was surprised and irritated by the way her stomach lurched at the sight of him and put it down to the suddenness of his appearance.

'Oh, hello. Fine, thanks.' She returned to pegging a jumper on the line.

'Don't suppose you've got any bookings yet, have you?'

Martin came closer, tipped his hat to the back of his head and regarded her with a twinkle in his eyes.

Helen sighed. Why could this man never mind his own business?

She tilted her chin and regarded him steadily. 'Actually I have, yes. Several.'

'Really?' His eyebrows rose. 'So you won't be selling your field yet then?' He was smiling, although she recognised the seriousness of the question.

She shook her head. 'Definitely not. I've applied for planning permission for the campsite. Even though I can't afford to get it under way just yet, it'll be ready for when I can.' She wrestled into the wind with a duvet cover and added, 'Your place seems to be coming along well.' She had noticed that men had started tiling the roof that morning.

'Yes, we're very pleased with it.' Martin glanced over his shoulder then added, 'I'm glad you've got Jack Roskilly doing your work, by the way.' He nodded towards the van with the builder's name painted on it which was parked nearby. 'He's one of the best in the trade. I would have recommended him to you myself — if I'd been asked.'

Helen was torn between annoyance at his patronising air and relief that he thought that she had chosen well — but why should it *matter* what he thought?

'I heard of his good reputation from another source,' she replied loftily, 'So all's well — 'Oh!' she cried as she lost her grip on the washing. The wind had won the battle and now merrily whisked the duvet cover over the hedge and almost into the building site. Then it dropped it playfully into the thickest of the brambles which were growing in the ditch at Martin's feet.

'Hard luck,' he said as he retrieved it, liberally plastered with muddy streaks. 'You'll have to wash this one again.' He rolled it up and jumped the hedge to pass it to her.

As their hands touched she felt a jolt like an electrical charge run up her arm and the unexpected shock of it made her terse reply sound little short of peevish. 'If you hadn't bundled it up with your dirty hands I might have been able to save it,' she grumbled. 'But thanks anyway.'

To her annoyance, Martin spread his impeccably clean palms for her inspection and looked her squarely in the eye. 'Not guilty,' he remarked.

Helen felt herself flush and was forced to apologise. Bending her head on the pretext of examining the cover, she muttered 'Sorry' under her breath and expected him to vault back over the hedge and go.

But not so. Like a drop of water wearing away a stone, he returned again to the subject of Helen's business as if there had been no interruption.

'Well, when you're up and running you'll need some help in the house, of course,' he remarked. 'You won't be able to handle everything yourself.'

'So I've already been told,' she said tartly, picking up the empty wash-basket.

'Ah, you've got somebody lined up, have you?'

Oh, why couldn't he just go away and mind his own business? And why was she incapable of telling him so? She tapped a toe on the ground in frustration and gritted her teeth.

Martin obviously took the silence for a negative reply, and went blithely on, 'It's just that I know just the person for you. My foreman's wife, Mary, has just lost her part-time work with the knitting factory closing down. They've got five children to support and she's desperate to find another job. This would be exactly right for her — and for you. I can vouch for her honesty and reliability — I've known her for years. I'll send her round to see you.' It wasn't a question, but a statement.

Pride fought with common sense as Helen's brain ticked furiously over. She was feeling unnerved by his proximity. His presence was making her on edge, and the fact that he was standing so close that their shoulders were almost touching made it hard for her to concentrate on what he was saying.

Was he this high-handed at home, she wondered? If so, his wife must be some kind of little mouse to put up with it. Although when she recalled the elegant woman she had briefly seen next door, she certainly hadn't fitted that description.

However, she had to concede that this Mary would certainly be the answer to one of her problems. She hadn't been looking forward to inter-viewing strangers. So yes, she sounded ideal, but the fact that it was all being organised for her and presented as a *fait accompli* by this disturbing man stuck in her throat.

Helen hastily averted her eyes from the muscular arm so near her own. The sleeves of his denim shirt were rolled partway up and the little dark hairs on his forearms were being touched with gold by the sun.

Forcing herself to concentrate, Helen raised her chin and tried to recover some of the dignity that she seemed to have lost.

'Well, all right, I suppose so. I'll see her, but I can't promise anything, of course. You'll make sure she understands that, won't you?'

She wanted to make sure they all knew where they stood in this situation. After all, she was calling the tune here — and she was doing him a favour, wasn't she?

Martin grinned and touched his forelock. 'Yes, ma'am, thank you, ma'am,' he replied. Was he making fun of her? Infuriating man!

She ignored the remark and with an effort stepped away from him.

She picked up the tin which held her clothes pegs and pushed it under the hedge where the wind couldn't upset it. Straightening up to go back indoors, she assumed that Martin would jump back over the hedge and return to his own side. To her amazement, however, he followed her down the path, still smiling.

'I'd like to just take a peek and see how your work's going while I'm here,' he said breezily. 'You don't mind, do you?' And he whistled a cheerful tune as he strode at her side, oblivious to her furious glare. How aggravating! For when he put it like that, Helen thought, how could she possibly say no?

\* \* \*

Hands on his hips, Martin surveyed the gap in what had been the dividing wall between the two rooms.

'Oh, yes,' he nodded, 'they've done a good job with that girder.' He thumped the wall with one hand and looked up at the new support above it.

'It's going to be finished off with an arch,' Helen volunteered. Now that he was here she supposed she might as well be civil.

'That'll look great. Just as if it's always been there.' He perched on a corner of the table and smiled as their eyes met. Then he fished in a pocket and pulled out a small object which he held up for her to see. 'I thought you might like to have this,' he said, 'as a companion piece to your Egyptian cat.'

Helen looked at the curio he was holding.

'What is it?' she asked blankly. It was a flat piece of what looked like stone glazed in green, a few inches long and broader than it was high, and was decorated with a single painted eye outlined in black.

'It's an amulet,' Martin replied. 'The ancient Egyptians wore them for good luck and for protection against evil spirits.'

'Oh, yes. And they placed them in their tombs to safeguard the dead in the after-life, didn't they?' she rejoined.

'That's right. This would have been worn around the neck on a leather thong. Look, you can see the loop where it would have been threaded.'

Helen drew close to see and a little shiver of heightened awareness feathered down her spine.

'This is the Eye of Horus,' Martin told her, handing it to her. 'One of the most common of all the images. Horus was supposed to bring strength, vigour, protection and safety to the wearer.'

'No wonder he was so popular,' Helen replied with a giggle. 'There's something there for everyone. Your all-purpose amulet, in fact — fits all sizes, every home should have one!' And there she was again, babbling away like a fool in order to cover her — what? — embarrassment was too strong a word. Awareness of this man's powerful charisma, possibly.

'Anyway,' Martin went on, 'I've had it for years and never do anything with it. I'd like you to have it. As a house-warming present, if you like, and to keep the statue of Bast company. They seem to be at home together. There.' While he'd been talking, he'd crossed the room and now stood the amulet on the natural shelf formed by the top edge of the sash window.

'They do make a good pair,' Helen agreed as she came to stand beside him. 'But I can't possibly accept it. It must be very valuable.'

'Oh, it's not an original,' he assured her. 'Don't worry about that. It's only a cheap copy that I picked up in one of the sales.'

'Well, if you're sure, then it's very kind of you. Thank you, I appreciate it.'

'They were a sort of pair in mythology actually,' Martin went on, stroking the statuette's head absently with one finger. 'Horus was one of the several sun-gods, and Bast, of course, was cat-headed.'

★   ★   ★

A knock at the door and a voice calling her name brought Helen back to earth.

'Oh, Tim, it's you. What a nice surprise!' She smiled as her brother let himself in and strode towards them, his bulk almost filling the narrow passage.

'Hi. I've been out on a job near Wheal Coates and I thought I'd pop in on the way back and see what you've been doing to this place of yours.' Tim brought with him a breath of the outdoors, with his shock of unruly hair ruffled by the sea-winds and his ruddy cheeks tanned by the sun.

'Lovely to see you, come in. This is Martin Somerville — he's building the bungalow next door. My brother, Tim.' The two men shook hands.

'I'll put the kettle on then,' she said when Martin showed no sign of leaving. Tim sat down on one of the kitchen chairs and they exchanged small-talk as Helen clattered mugs and spoons on the worktop.

'It's looking good, Helen,' said Tim, nodding approval as he looked around the room. 'It's made a huge difference, knocking through like that.'

'Glad you like it,' said his sister, passing them each a mug.

'I'll tell you my plans for the campsite sometime as well.' She had no wish to discuss the subject in front of Martin, however pleasant he was making himself. 'I've applied for outline permission, did I tell you? But I'll have to get a professional in at some point, of course.'

'I think you'd be wise to concentrate on one thing at a time,' Tim remarked, sipping his tea. 'Best see how the B and B works out first, eh?'

'Oh, I am,' Helen replied. 'I haven't got the money to do anything else. And I'm not looking forward to old Roskilly's bill for this lot.' She nodded towards the alterations.

'Oh, I almost forgot.' Tim put down his mug and rummaged in an inside pocket of his fleece jacket. 'Mum asked me to give you this.' He pulled out a large envelope. 'She says it's the letters and stuff of Aunt Grace's that you wanted. There isn't much, but you can keep them, she says — she doesn't want anything back.'

'Ooh, lovely!' Helen took it with enthusiasm. 'Martin and I were just looking at that. She pointed to the amulet which was glowing with colour in the light coming in through the open window. 'Oh, you tell him what it is, Martin, will you? I want to see what's in here.' She turned over the envelope and shook out its contents.

'Sure.' He rose and went to the window, taking down the charm which he brought back to the table and handed to Tim with an explanation.

'We were talking about your aunt and how she must have spent time in Egypt,' he added.

Tim handed back the charm and

Martin crossed the room to put it back in the window.

'Oh, yeah, Aunt Grace was a bit of an eccentric, from what I can remember of her,' said Tim. 'She was quite old when we were children, tall and still straight-backed. Pencil-thin too. And she had a very brown and wrinkled face, didn't she? That would be from all the Egyptian sun, I suppose. I imagine she was quite a character in her day. That right, Helen?'

She nodded. 'I always got that impression too. Mainly because we were never told much about her — which makes me think that she might have got up to things that weren't suitable for our childish ears!' She grinned, raising her head from the papers in her hand. 'There's more stuff here than I thought. I'll have to go through it all another time. Tell Mum thanks, Tim, and I'll phone her sometime.'

'Well, I must be off.' Martin glanced at his watch and picked up his hard-hat which he had hooked on the back of his chair. 'I'm supposed to be working. Thanks for the tea, Helen. See you around. Bye, Tim.'

'He seems a nice chap,' Tim remarked as Helen came back from seeing Martin out.

'He's all right, I suppose,' she replied, gathering up the used mugs and turning towards the sink.

'You don't sound very enthusiastic.' He shot her a penetrating look. 'He seemed very friendly, I thought. And he gave you the amulet,' he pointed out.

She gave a shrug. 'He's very full of his own importance too,' she retorted.

'Well, you like him enough to ask him in for tea, so he can't be that bad,' her brother replied with a grin.

'But I *didn't* ask him,' Helen protested. 'He just kind of . . . followed me in after we'd been talking outside.'

She could hear herself how feeble this sounded and wasn't surprised at her brother's sardonic snort of amusement.

'Besides, he's married with a family,' she said firmly. 'We're going to be neighbours, so I don't want to antagonise him, that's all.'

'I see,' said Tim, pushing back his chair. 'Can I take a walk up over your field while I'm here? Might as well see the whole of the estate, eh?'

'Sure,' Helen replied. 'Not that there's much to see. Mining remains and a lot of overgrown weeds, that's it really. But one day . . . '

She was interrupted by the phone. 'You go on, Tim — I'll catch you up in a minute,' she said, going to answer it.

To her delight it was another enquiry about a holiday booking, and by the time she'd answered all the woman's questions and established that the two weeks which she wanted were available, her brother was back again.

'Sorry about that,' Helen said with a smile. 'It was business. Another booking!' And she pencilled in the date on the calendar beside her, to be verified in writing later on.

'Well, I must be off now,' said her brother. He was wearing a preoccupied look and didn't respond to her remark. 'Take care of yourself, Helen. See you again soon.'

'You too,' she replied. 'Bye.'

She stayed on the step as he went down the path, but he still appeared to be sunk in his own thoughts and didn't look back.

★ ★ ★

'I've got a bit of a problem with all this furniture,' said Helen to the builders a few days later.

Jack and his son were ready to start work on the small boxroom, but it would have to be cleared before they could even get over the threshold. This was in spite of the fact that she had already packed up masses of smaller things, which had included among the bric-a-brac many souvenirs and mementoes of her great-aunt's travels.

'I don't want to get rid of it entirely

in case I need some of it later on.'
She spread her hands and shrugged.
'So I thought it could go out in the
garage until I decide. I don't mind
leaving the car outside now that the
weather's improving. But I can't move
it on my own and I don't know who
to ask for help.' She turned appealing
eyes on the two men. 'So I was
wondering — I know it's a lot to ask
— but . . . '

'Oh, we'll soon shift it for you, my
'andsome,' said Jack with a grin.
'Nothing to it. Come us on, Ted, you
take the drawers out of that chest and
we'll carry them out separate like. I'll
get this here out of the way.' He turned
his attention to a large cupboard and
grasped the side of it with a fist the size
of a small ham. 'Out in the garage you
said?'

Helen nodded. 'Please.'

'No trouble. Right, steady as we go,
boy, mind that there corner . . . '

The room was cleared in half an
hour, then, fortified with huge mugs of

tea, the two men began work soon afterwards.

Helen closed the door and left them to it while she climbed the open staircase to her own room. The envelope of photos and letters which Tim had brought was lying on her desk and now she had time to look at them properly.

She took them downstairs, settled herself and tipped out the contents.

The photos were all of a young woman who could only have been Grace, taken at various places she must have visited on her travels. Her face alight with interest, Helen skimmed through them. Here was Grace gazing out over Niagara Falls; in another one she was with a group of friends, screwing up her eyes against the sun with the Taj Mahal in the background. This must be Venice, for there were gondolas tied to striped mooring poles, and, yes, there were the pyramids at Giza and the unmistakable image of the Sphinx.

The rest of the photos seemed to be all of Egypt. There were feluccas sailing on the Nile, with parrots and palm trees in the background. Loaded camels, their drovers wearing white turbans and long tunics, holding fly-whisks at the ready. Groups of people, posing with native guides beside pyramids, temples, statues and tombs.

She flicked through them all, then spent time going through them more slowly one by one, squinting as she tried to decipher the cramped and faded handwriting on the backs.

After a few minutes, however, she sighed in frustration. She'd need a magnifying glass if she was ever going to read any of this, and that was something she didn't possess. She rose to her feet and pushed back her chair in exasperation, at the same moment as the doorbell rang.

She was surprised to find Martin standing on the step. A soft thin rain was falling today and the view was partially obscured by a veil of drifting mist. Beads of moisture glistened on his hair and his waxed jacket was dripping onto the doormat.

'Hi,' he said with a grin. 'I thought you might like to borrow this.' He fished into a deep pocket and pulled out a book which he handed to her.

'*Myths and Legends of Ancient Egypt*,' she read on the cover and smiled up at him. 'Oh, yes, thanks. I'd love to.' Then, realising that the rain was getting heavier and was driving into the house, she had no option but to say, 'Won't you come in?' hoping that he had pressing business to attend to elsewhere and would decline.

No such luck. 'Thanks,' he said and stepped into the passage. He slipped off his jacket and hung it on the nearest peg before following her into the sitting-room.

★ ★ ★

Through the picture window they could see the great woolly clouds of mist clearly now, as they came sweeping in across the bay on the back of a soft south westerly wind.

'Quite a change,' said Martin as he peered out. 'I'm not sorry to stay indoors today. I'm waiting for some plaster to dry, so I can afford a day off.'

'It's supposed to clear later, according to the forecast,' Helen replied. 'I was just looking at these photos that Tim brought over. A lot of them were taken in Egypt.' She passed a couple over to him. 'Oh — I don't suppose by any chance you've got a magnifying glass, have you? I was trying to read Grace's handwriting on the back of these, and I can't make it out — most of it's quite faded and it's very small.'

'I've got one in the car actually.' He sat up and glanced out of the window. 'When it stops chucking it down I'll nip out and fetch it. I keep it for reading maps. Hey, these are interesting, aren't they? Is that your aunt there?'

Helen nodded and smiled. 'Yes, that's Grace all right. She was always the tallest one in any group, which makes it easy to pick her out in a crowd. Here she is with the Sphinx in the background.'

'Did you know that the Sphinx is a monument to Horus?' Martin remarked as he peered more closely at the little square print.

Helen shook her head. 'No — really?'

'Yes, there's a small shrine to him there — in between its paws actually.' He smiled. 'Oh, and there they are at the Temple of Horus at Edfu,' he added, pointing. 'I recognise it from that book. Isn't that a coincidence?' He turned to her with a smile. 'Can you see the painted eye motif, just there?

Helen bent nearer and their shoulders brushed. 'Mm,' she replied, very conscious of Martin's warm breath in her hair, and hastily withdrew.

To give her hands something to do, she picked up the book of myths which he had brought and began to flip through its index. Her interest in Horus having been aroused, she would see what the book had to say about him.

"Horus, son of Osiris," she read aloud. "One of the best-loved of the Egyptian gods. He represented the sun, and the rays of light which fell from his eye nourished life on earth. He was always at war with Set, the god of darkness. Together they also symbolised the forces of good and evil . . . "

She looked up from the page and smiled. 'This is interesting stuff,' she said.

'See what it says about Bast while you're there,' he replied, and Helen turned to the index once more.

' 'Bast had her temple at the city of Bubastis where she was worshipped and where her festival took place during April and May, the fertile months of the year. Thus the fertility of the animal became associated with the moon, which typified the ideals of fruitfulness and growth.'' Helen grinned. 'As anyone who has heard alley-cats screeching at night can believe.'

She closed the book and looked up in

surprise as she heard a knock and Jack Roskilly put his head around the half-open door.

'Just came to give you this,' he said, holding up a dusty cardboard folder. 'We found it down behind that cupboard when we moved it. Caught underneath, it was. There's some pictures or something inside,' he added.

'Oh, thanks very much, Jack,' she said as he withdrew.

'I wonder what it is?' she muttered, more to herself than to Martin, as she placed it on a side table and bent to undo the faded ribbon with which it was fastened.

Martin came and looked over her shoulder as she drew out some of the sheets of paper that it held.

'Wow!' they both said together.

'Paintings!' Helen exclaimed. 'Original paintings — I didn't know Aunt Grace was an artist.'

Very carefully, she took out some more and laid them out on the carpet at their feet.

Martin was watching intently as she added several others. 'These are really good,' he said with enthusiasm.

'And they're all illustrations of Egypt, or Egyptian things,' Helen added. 'Look at these hieroglyphics, how detailed they are . . . '

'And the figures on the wall here — that must be from one of the tombs, I should think. Aren't they perfect?'

'So are the outdoor scenes, too. Look at those camels with their noses in the air!'

'Here's the Sphinx, and the Pyramids — and see those two pillars there with all the carvings? The detail she's put in! She was very talented, your aunt.'

Kneeling on the floor they picked up sheet after sheet of the colourful scenes, still jewel-bright even after their long incarceration in the dust underneath the cupboard.

'I'm surprised no-one knew that she was an artist.' Helen sat back on her heels and looked puzzled. 'At least, no one ever told me, and I can't remember ever seeing any of her work before.'

'There's a bundle of smaller sketches here,' Martin said, picking one up. 'They look like images of local people, I should think. Here's a chap in a long white robe and turban. He's the camel drover, and he's looking over his shoulder and grinning as if he knew he was being painted.'

'That's strange,' Helen remarked as she riffled through some more of the smaller sketches and passed them over for Martin to see. 'These are *all* of that same person — the man driving the camels. Full-face, close-up, in profile . . . ' She went through them one at a time. 'With the Sphinx in the background, head and shoulders, holding one of his camels . . . Isn't that strange?'

Martin shrugged. 'Perhaps he was just very — not photogenic — but whatever the word is for drawing — 'sketchable'?' and they laughed together.

'Wait a minute,' said Helen suddenly.

'I've just thought of something.' She scrambled to her feet and went back to the photos that she had been looking at before the interruption.

'Come and look at these.'

He joined her at the table as she picked up the bundle of pictures and passed them to him.

'Do you notice anything?'

Martin looked at each one in turn and then turned to her with wonder in his eyes. 'The same man! In every single one.'

'In the group pictures, along with the visitors. With his camels in the background in the local scenes. And in this one outside the hotel, he's even in the group photo,' Helen pointed. 'And *he's standing next to Grace*! What do you think of that?'

Martin grinned. 'The same as you're thinking, I'm sure.'

'That they had an *affair*?' Helen's eyes widened. 'Wow, I wonder? Gosh — Aunt Grace! The last person I would have imagined. From what I remember she was the soul of propriety.'

She turned to Martin, her face a picture of amazement. 'To have an affair at all in those days was pretty scandalous — but with a '*native*' — ' she sketched a couple of quotation marks in the air. ' — that would mean the end of her career, and of any chance of being accepted in society ever again.'

'Good for her, I say,' Martin replied. 'She must have been one spirited lady. Not unlike one of her descendants whom I happen to know.' Their eyes met for a long moment and his face had become suddenly sober.

★   ★   ★

Helen dragged her gaze away and glanced out of the window. 'Look, it's stopped raining at last,' she said to change the subject. 'See how the sky's lightening out over the sea.' The curtain of rain had parted and a snippet of pearly sky had appeared on the horizon. Gaining in strength by the minute, a

114

pale sun was emerging and gilding the swell of the waves as the breeze freshened and dispelled the last of the mist.

'Right.' Martin rose to his feet. 'I'll go and get that magnifying glass now.'

Helen followed him to the door and watched as he ran into the next-door driveway and returned.

'*Et voila!*' he said, grinning as he passed the magnifying glass to her with a flourish.

'Thanks,' said Helen, wondering whether he was coming back in again or not.

'Keep it for as long as you need, I'm in no hurry for it back.' He paused, then looked up the garden and jerked his head towards the back of the house. 'I was wondering, while I'm here, whether — well, the fact is — I'd love to walk up to your field and have a look at where it joins my land. I've never seen it from the other side, you see. The hedge is too high. Would you mind?'

'No . . . no, I suppose not.' Helen

was instantly suspicious, knowing of his business interest in her land, but could think of no logical reason why she should refuse. 'Just let me get my wellies — the grass will be soaking wet.'

They walked around to the back of the house, through a small gate, and climbed the steep slope of rough grass where a couple of black goats raised their heads, regarded them curiously with intelligent amber eyes, then went on grazing unperturbed.

'They'll have to go eventually, of course,' Helen remarked, 'but at the moment they're doing a grand job of mowing the grass for me.'

They reached the top of the slope where the grass gave way to a patch of derelict land strewn with loose stones and the ruins of old mining buildings.

'There was experimental mining here, I believe, at one time,' Helen told Martin. 'I'm told that a couple of shafts were sunk but they didn't find anything worth developing and it was abandoned, leaving all this mess behind. I know I'm leaping ahead but I thought that one day I might plant this up with shrubs and trees. It would hide the debris and make a feature of this bit of land.'

While she was talking, Martin was pushing his way through the tangle of brambles and other wild plants which had taken over the fallen masonry and were making their own attempt to clothe it with greenery.

'Looking at all this stuff reminds me,' he said, waving a hand around. 'Did you see that article in the local paper about some miraculous plant that absorbs arsenic from the soil and kind of cleans it up? I thought it was a joke at first, but it wasn't April Fool's Day, so I guess it was for real.'

Helen giggled. 'No, I didn't see it in the paper,' she replied, 'but Tim told me all about it. His department is very involved. I thought he was winding me up at first, too, but it's perfectly true. It sounded a bit creepy to me, like something from outer space.'

It was as they were turning to go back that she caught the toe of her Wellington boot on one of the loose stones and stumbled. It seemed that she was heading for a fall, but Martin caught her to save her.

'Oh! Thanks!' she stammered.

'Are you all right?' Anxious dark eyes looked into her face as she tried to regain her composure, her heart hammering against her ribs.

She managed to nod and say weakly, 'I — I tripped. It's these boots — they're too big for me really.'

She sagged against him, managing to joke. 'This is the second time I've fallen into your arms!'

She told herself she should move, but the shoulder upon which she was resting her head was very warm and incredibly soothing. It was clad in a soft sweater of muted greens and browns and she realised with a start that she had been needing a strong supporting arm like this for a long time. The proverbial shoulder to cry on, in fact. Since leaving Alex, she'd missed his companionship and friendship, and had been subconsciously lacking the comfort that is brought about by the physical touch of another person.

Then cold realisation hit her. What on earth was she doing? This was another woman's husband, for goodness' sake! With an effort, she jerked herself free and took a step away from him. He looked startled and slightly bewildered as she said brusquely, 'Thank you, I'll be all right now.'

They began to walk slowly back towards the house.

'Are you coming in again to see the rest of the photos?' Helen asked in order to change the subject.

'No, thanks. Let me know if you find anything else interesting though.' When he declined, Helen felt a little stab of disappointment that surprised her. She waved goodbye as he went through the gate and remained where she was, watching the departing car until it rounded a bend and was out of sight.

★ ★ ★

Lost in thought, she came to with a start and realised that the phone was ringing. She ran inside and snatched up the receiver.

'Oh, Jane, it's you!' she gasped.

'You took your time answering,' said her friend. 'Where were you?'

'Outside. Martin was here and he was just saying goodbye.'

'Martin? Martin Somerville, you mean? But I thought you were at daggers drawn with him? What's happened that you're so friendly all of a sudden? Something I don't know about?'

'Oh, there's a lot to tell you, but no, nothing like that — he's married with a family. But he's much nicer than I thought at first . . . '

She launched into a long chat with

her friend which brought her up to date with all the latest developments.

'And the renovations are almost finished,' she added. 'Of course, I can't afford to tackle the campsite this year. I could do with the money, but the goats will have to have it to themselves for a bit longer.'

'Have you got any bookings for the B and B yet?' Jane asked. 'I want to come down myself for a week in September. Make sure you save me some time and let me know which week I can have, OK?'

'Great! Of course I will.'

As they said their goodbyes and she put the phone down, Helen mused wistfully that September was a long way off. It was still only February and she could have done with her friend's cheerful company right now.

But keeping busy was the best way to shake off the blues, she told herself, firmly, and there was certainly plenty to do. On that thought she went out to the garage to fetch the emulsion paint she had bought for the newly refurbished small bedroom.

* * *

Over the next few days as she climbed up and down stepladders, struggled with paint-rollers and brushes and ached in muscles she hadn't known she possessed, Helen wondered whether this scheme had been the best of ideas after all. But by pampering her battered body in several hot soaks liberally laced with scented bath oil she managed to survive physically, and the sight of the amazing improvement of the house due to her own efforts was so encouraging that it spurred her on when she felt more like dropping her tools where they were and collapsing into bed.

At last the alterations downstairs were finished and the builders departed. Helen breathed a sigh of relief at finally having the place to herself and looked around her with satisfaction. Having the work done had definitely been the right decision. It had transformed the original small and rather dark kitchen into an elegant breakfast-room and partitioned cooking area, just as she had imagined.

A thrill of excitement ran through her. In her mind's eye, she could see the room filled with eager, animated holidaymakers and herself flitting to and fro, serving them all perfectly-cooked breakfasts, a smile on her face, the 'hostess with the mostest'. She couldn't wait for Jane to come and see how different it all looked.

But first things first. Before she did anything else, the whole house would need a thorough clean from top to bottom, to get rid of all the cement dust which was covering everything.

It was going to take some considerable time but she decided that there was no need to waste money on employing someone to do what she could manage perfectly well herself, so she set to and polished windows, dusted corners, vacuumed carpets, until her back ached and her throat was as dry as dust itself.

It seemed that she would never see the end of the dust — as soon as she cleaned one area, she'd open a door and another cloud would fly in. It was an extremely frustrating job but at last it was finished and as she took a final look around her gleaming home, she didn't regret a thing.

Now for the furnishings! This was what she'd been waiting for! She jumped into the car and set off on a final shopping trip for new curtains, duvet covers and towels to finish off the guestrooms. The last big item was the set of new bunk beds for the children's room.

At last everything was organised. As she might have expected, she'd over-spent her budget and had an overdraft at the bank, but now wasn't the time to worry about that. The important thing, after all, was that she was ready to open for business — and in time for the start of the holiday season, too.

# A Monumental Mistake

Easter came early that year, towards the end of March, and Helen was kept pleasingly busy with her visitors. Fortunately the weather was good, the sea calm and inviting, if not quite warm enough for bathing, while inland the hedges were full of primroses and brilliant pink campions. Bluebells carpeted the woods and creamy cow parsley frothed in the ditches, while the sun smiled down as if on cue.

Most of her visitors were families who were content to enjoy the beach and the breathtaking scenery of the coastal walks nearby. For older people and those with more cultural tastes there were plenty of places within driving distance for them to visit. The Tate Gallery at St Ives, the newly-opened Maritime Museum at Falmouth and the world famous Eden Project near St Austell all offered attractive days out.

After her current guests had all departed one morning, she raised her head from the mammoth pile of washing-up that faced her every day and reached for yet another tea-towel.

'Mary, the first thing I'm going to treat myself to when I've got some spare cash is a dishwasher,' she said with feeling and the other woman looked over her shoulder and laughed.

Mary Harris was proving to be a real treasure, and grudgingly Helen had to admit that she should be grateful to Martin for suggesting her. Mid-forties, she guessed, completely unflappable and always cheerful, Mary was willing to turn her hand to anything and was only too delighted to have been taken on.

'Jobs are so scarce around here — especially part-time ones,' she'd said the other day as she tackled a pile of ironing. 'When all the students come down in the summer they snap them up, you know. I never thought I'd be as lucky as this.' She tested the heat of the iron with the flat of her hand. 'It's the mortgage, you see. We'd never be able to keep up the payments unless I had a bit of work.'

'Well, this will tide you over the summer months,' Helen replied, 'but you do realise that I may not need your help during the winter?'

Best to make that clear at the outset, she thought to herself. She would have to save every penny she could after the holiday season was over.

Mary nodded. 'Of course I do. Maybe something else will turn up by then, unexpected like, same as this did. Anyhow, I'll worry about that when the time do come.' She smiled placidly and hung a couple of pillowcases over the back of a chair to air off.

'How nice it must be not to worry about things,' Helen remarked. 'I seem to spend half my time fretting over what might go wrong. But I suppose it's inborn, not something we can learn.'

Mary smiled. 'Wouldn't do if we were all alike now, would it? Make for a dull old world, that would.'

Fetching a pile of linen from the airing cupboard she said, 'I'll go and tackle the beds next, shall I? Then I'll get the cleaner out and sweep up a bit.'

'Thanks,' Helen replied. 'I've got to go into Truro and stock up on food, but I shan't be long.'

She set off with a spring in her step. Everything was going so well she could hardly believe it. Here she was, the 'seaside landlady' that Jane had joked about just a few short months ago.

With a flip of excitement she realised that she had made a success of a dream. Hadn't she? She crossed her fingers, hardly able to believe it. But once she'd paid off her debts and recouped her outlay, she could see no reason why it shouldn't continue. And she gave a little smile of satisfaction.

★　★　★

Helen was humming softly along with the radio as she picked up the post from the mat one morning. Most of it was junk, but her heart started thumping faster as she came across an official one stamped with the emblem of the district council.

Tearing it open, she skimmed its contents.

She gasped and her hand flew to her mouth as she took in the message, then read it slowly through a second time to make sure she had got it right.

'. . . *must refuse permission to erect buildings on your property for the purpose of creating a campsite on your land . . . in an area which has recently been declared a Site of Special Scientific Interest . . . A report of a rare plant, namely Pteris cretica, or Cretan fern, has been received by us and we regret that building on this site is therefore out of the question . . . Should you wish to lodge an appeal, or discuss this further . . . contact . . .*'

Permission refused! Because of a

dratted *plant!* And, what's more, the arsenic-eating fern which had seemed such a joke when she had first heard of it. Surely part of her dream couldn't be crumbling to nothing almost before it had even begun! She stared at the paper, numb with shock, the words dancing in front of her eyes and blinding her to their sense.

Then her brain clicked into gear and she started to think about it logically. How had they found out? That was the first question. She looked at the letter again. ' . . . a report has been received . . . ' She nibbled a thumb, her mind reeling. No-one had ever asked for her permission to look around that field. And no-one could have got into it unless they had sneaked up there when she was away from home. There was no other access than by her own garden. So who . . . ?

Realisation hit her with the force of a ton of bricks, and her stomach lurched. Martin Somerville! That was who! Wasn't it? It had to be. What was it he had said? 'I'd like to have a look at the field from your side . . . ' or something like that. And he had poked about among all the undergrowth and — yes — he had actually said something about the fern then! She hadn't thought anything of it at the time. Oh, the *rat!* The low-down scheming *louse!*

Helen slumped into a chair, fury flaming her face. Then fury gave way to tears of hurt and frustration which streamed down her cheeks in a hot torrent. How could he betray her so?

Her lip trembled as she thought of the tenuous friendship that she'd thought had recently sprung up between them. He had seemed so nice as she got to know him a little better. But obviously her first impression of him had been the right one — he was a self-seeking, money-grubbing *rat!* Of course he would have put his own interests first, she fumed. He had always had an eye on her land and was apparently ruthless enough to sink to any level to get his own way. This letter from the council proved it!

Her head reeling over this new turn of events, she sagged in the chair, feeling about as low as she could get as all her worst fears reared up to confront her.

In debt as she was, and with no prospect now of being able to expand the business, she was going to have to get a job in the quiet period between Easter and the summer season and try to recoup her losses. And that wouldn't be easy, as Mary Harris had pointed out.

But searing into her soul more deeply than anything else was the matter of Martin Somerville's blatant betrayal. The more she thought about that stab in the back, the more churned up her feelings became.

She rose to her feet and paced the room, unable to settle to anything.

Could she put in an appeal to the authorities, emphasising her position, explaining to them how desperately she needed to develop her land? She could try, but in her heart of hearts she doubted it would make any difference.

Could she suggest that the con-founded fern be moved to somewhere else? That was a thought, and her face brightened momentarily. It was a possibility, but against the might of the council plus the body — whoever they were — that looked after listed sites, what chance did she have?

* * *

A few days passed during which Helen took a preliminary trip to the job centre to see what was on offer and drew a complete blank. Unless she wanted to slave long hours for the very basic minimum wage, there was nothing remotely suitable, and she came home feeling lower than ever.

Then one morning she happened to glance out of the window and there he was, Martin Somerville, with his back towards her and a spade in his hand, starting to dig over his garden.

Her stomach lurched, then her

mouth set into a determined line. Straightening her shoulders, she took a deep breath and marched outside.

'Hey, I want a word with you!' she called over the hedge.

Martin jumped at the sound of her voice, then turned towards her with a broad smile.

'Hi.' He stuck the spade in the soil and walked over. 'Haven't seen you for a while. I've been kept pretty busy at our new site. How's business?' His voice was bland and composed and he looked perfectly at ease. How *could* he? Helen fumed.

'And which site would that be?' she snapped. 'I've heard how busy you've been on mine.'

'What?' His brow puckered. 'Sorry, I don't follow you.'

'You louse!' Helen spat. 'How could you do such a thing? You underhand, conniving, low-down rat! Why couldn't you have told me first before going to the council? Don't I have the right to that much consideration?'

He stared at her with plain astonishment. 'What on earth are you talking about? Louse? Rat? What am I supposed to have done, for goodness' sake?' His face was grim now and the smiling eyes had turned dangerously dark.

'I don't believe this! You have the nerve to stand there and try to tell me you don't know?' She knew she was sounding like a fish-wife but she was too incensed to care. 'You rotten, two-faced . . . words fail me, they really do.'

'Well, that has to be a welcome change,' came the sarcastic reply. 'In that case, I'll get back to work.' And he turned his back and strode away.

Helen was left with her mouth open, totally deflated, feeling more foolish than she had ever felt in her life. Why didn't he stand up for himself — argue — protest — deny it?

Because it was all true, of course, whispered a small inner voice. What else could he say? And slowly the remaining faint hope that she might have got it wrong, might possibly have misjudged him, crumbled to dust and blew away on the brisk sea breeze.

She watched as Martin took up the spade again, hesitated, then jabbed it forcefully into the soil with some muttered expletive. Then he marched purposefully out of his gate, in through hers and up the path towards her.

Transfixed, Helen could only wait as he came closer until they were standing within a few feet of each other. His face was twisted with fury and his eyes flashed angry sparks.

'I thought I could ignore all that,' he said through gritted teeth. 'I tried hard to rise above it in an adult manner. Don't let the ravings of a hysterical woman get to you, I told myself. But I can't take insults like that lying down — and why should I?'

His face was very near her own, so close that Helen could breathe in the scent of his skin. There was a crisp scent of peppermint about it, mingled with some fragrance of the aftershave that he used, fresh and attractive.

'What on earth was it all about?' He glowered down at her, his eyes boring into her.

Helen found her voice at last and retorted, 'Don't try to pretend you don't know! You went to the council and reported that I had that blasted fern growing on my land. It must have been you because nobody else knows . . . and . . . and now they've refused p-planning p-permission . . . ' To her horror her voice suddenly broke and huge sobs racked her body.

Martin's brows shot up to his hairline and his mouth dropped open in astonishment. '*Me?* You seriously think that *I* — ' he jabbed his chest with a forefinger ' — would do something so underhand to *you?* That I would deliberately land you in trouble? Why on earth should I do that? What do you take me for, for goodness' sake?'

Through her tears Helen saw the bewilderment on his face. It had to be genuine, she thought with horror. He meant what he was saying. Her stomach turned over. She'd made a dreadful mistake, hadn't she?

The shock dried up her tears in an instant. Feeling all sorts of a fool, she stammered, 'But I thought you'd done it so that you could get the land you want — so that I'd have to sell up like you said and — and . . . But you didn't, did you?' She hung her head and nibbled her bottom lip, wishing the earth would open and swallow her up.

To her amazement she heard him chuckle softly and felt a finger under her chin, lifting it until she had no choice but to meet his eyes — eyes that were now as soft and gentle as they had been stormy a moment ago.

'Oh, you poor, mixed-up little thing,' he whispered, as both arms encircled her in a gentle clasp. Then his mouth was on hers, fastening on her lips in a warm and passionate kiss which left her breathless.

Caught unawares, the shock of it left

her limp and helpless, while at the same time a host of conflicting feelings were fighting in her mind. Anguish, hurt, frustration, fury. Chief of them was fury. Here he was, a married man, and he could make a blatant pass at her like this! What did that make her in his eyes? An easy catch? The arrogance of it! And if he could betray his wife so readily, how could she possibly believe that he hadn't betrayed her as well?

Tears of anger and, yes, disappointment — she admitted that much — flooded her eyes again as she wrenched herself free, took a step back and slapped his face as hard as she could.

Martin's jaw dropped and he turned white with shock as his hand flew to his cheek. He opened his mouth to speak but Helen got in first.

'How *dare* you!' she exclaimed. 'What do you take me for, you arrogant, two-timing . . . Oh! I never want to see you again!' And she was off, ignoring his shout, running for the house as fast as her shaking legs would carry her.

Panting and sobbing, she hurled herself inside and slammed the door shut behind her. She leaned against it for support but her legs refused to hold her and she slid slowly to the floor, collapsing in a tearful heap on the mat.

★ ★ ★

Helen only managed to struggle through the next few days by blotting the whole dreadful scene out of her mind and throwing herself into her work. Shopping, answering enquiries, handling deposits, looking after the paying guests, writing receipts and keeping accounts were enough to keep her occupied, apart from the domestic side of things which she shared with Mary Harris.

But when she put out the light at last and climbed into bed each night, it would all surface to haunt her and deprive her of the sleep she desperately needed. Her reflection in the mirror looked sickly back at her. Her cheeks had a hollow look to them and there were dark shadows under her eyes.

When she answered the door one afternoon to find her mother standing on the step, Laura's opening remarks did nothing to make her feel any better.

'You look terrible!' she exclaimed.

'Hello, Mum, come in,' Helen said dully.

Laura stepped in and stared critically at her. As usual, she looked immaculate herself, wearing a smart navy jacket over a floral skirt in a neat print, and with every hair in place.

'Helen — what a mess you are!'

'Don't wrap it up, will you?' Helen replied with mock-humour, putting the kettle on and rattling china. She had been sweeping down the back yard and washing the blown salt off the windows, and was wearing the old trousers and torn shirt that she kept especially for dirty jobs.

Laura sat down on a kitchen chair and clicked open a compact mirror, giving her own face a reassuring glance. She dabbed a little powder on her nose, snapped the compact shut and returned it to her bag.

'It's all too much for you, isn't it?' she said as she looked with distaste at the mug in which Helen had served her tea. 'I told you you'd taken on more than you could handle, remember? And now look at you — it's dragging you down and you're completely worn out.'

Helen kept her temper with difficulty. She was already on a short fuse and it wouldn't take very much to set it off.

'I haven't been sleeping well, that's all. The business is doing just fine. We were fully booked over Easter and the summer is looking promising too,' she replied with defiance.

'Hmm,' Laura replied. 'That's all very well, but if your health is going to suffer, I just don't think it's worth it. You're still a young woman and your looks are important if you want to . . .'

. . . if I want to attract a man, Helen added silently, and seethed as she glared at her mother.

'I'm on my way into Truro to do some shopping, so I thought I'd call in and see your little place,' Laura went on. 'But if we're only going to squabble . . .'

Helen sighed and made a big effort to be pleasant. 'I'm really glad to see you,' she lied. 'Come and have a look at the new bedroom. I decorated it myself.'

'Mm, very nice dear,' said Laura, looking around the pink-washed walls and bright curtains. 'Although I always did prefer wallpaper — especially in a bedroom. I think it looks more cosy somehow. But yet, you've done a good job.' For you. The words hung in the air unspoken and Helen gritted her teeth together so that they remained unsaid.

'Would you like a walk up to the field?' she asked as they returned downstairs. 'I'll show you what I plan to do with it.'

As they picked their way through the long grass and fallen stones with care, both very aware of her mother's dainty high-heeled shoes, Laura remarked, 'I remember Grace had quite a nice garden here years ago. She was very keen on gardening after she retired — when she was at home long enough to tend to it, that is.'

Laura waved her hands expressively. 'She had statuary dotted around, and all sorts of curious things that she'd picked up on her travels. And beautiful flower-beds.' She turned to Helen. 'You don't remember that, I suppose?'

Helen shook her head. 'No, I don't. I was away for so many years, of course, what with college and then work.'

'Yes, you would have been. And now there's nothing left to see.'

'Maybe in years to come, when I get the time, I'll try to restore it.' Helen smiled. 'But I expect I shall be ready for retirement myself before I get round to it.'

After they had returned indoors, they chatted about Grace for a while longer as they sipped their tea, then the conversation turned to generalities and the rest of Laura's visit passed more pleasantly than it had begun.

Eventually Laura put down her mug, glanced at it with a look of faint distaste and consulted the gold watch on her wrist.

'Well, this has been nice but I must go,' she said, rising to her feet.

Helen uttered a few more pleasantries, then waved her mother off and turned back into the house with a sigh of relief.

Deciding that she needed a breath of fresh air after being indoors and trying to be sociable, she wandered out of the back door and headed toward the field again. A garden, Mum had said. Statuary. Helen wondered if there were any signs of it left that she might have overlooked.

Then she recalled the stone she had tripped over when — when . . . yes, well. It had been about halfway down the field, away from the mining debris, about — about here.

Helen bent down and peered into the long grass by the hedge.

There it was. She stood up and poked at it with her foot. It was heavy, too heavy to lever upwards that way. She stooped and heaved with both hands. Gradually it moved and came away from its bed in the soft soil. She turned it over — and had the surprise of her life. For as she rubbed away at the surface dirt she revealed a perfect model of the Sphinx. Complete in every detail, not chipped or worn from its long interment in the soil, it was instantly recognisable.

Her first reaction was that she must tell Martin. 'Let me know if you find anything else that's interesting,' he'd said. Then her face fell as she remembered . . .

\* \* \*

Over the next few weeks, Helen was forced to take a realistic look at the situation she was in. Without the prospect of some future income from the campsite, there was no way she was going to be able to continue with her business. Basically the house was just too small. With only three bedrooms it was never going to be a viable proposition on its own, and there was no space outside to add on an extension even if she could have afforded to do so.

The problem haunted her day and night and she eventually came to the conclusion that she had a stark choice. She could sell up and go back to London where she could earn good money again, but that would mean killing the dream and breaking her own heart. Or she could not sell up but rent out the house while she was in London and so hang on to the possibility of returning at some time in the future.

That would not be quite so drastic, but it would mean that she would have to employ somebody — either an agency or perhaps Mary Harris — to look after the house while she was away.

But if she did that, would the income

be worth all the worry of maintaining the place from such a distance?

And more importantly, would the rent money combined with the salary she would be getting be enough to pay off her overdraft as well as enabling her to live in London where everything cost so much more?

Figures writhed round and round in her head until it felt fit to burst, but finally she came to the conclusion that selling up was the obvious answer. Put the whole thing on the market as soon as possible. So the rat would get his field just as he had predicted and she would have to bury her dream for ever.

Unaware that she was nibbling a thumbnail and gazing out of the window at nothing, she was brought back to earth with a start as she realised that Mary had been speaking to her and she hadn't taken in a word of it. As she came out of her reverie with a jerk, her elbow caught the Eye of Horus, toppling it from its perch and on to the floor.

Well, that had to be symbolic if ever anything was, Helen thought, not knowing whether to laugh or cry as she bent to retrieve it. Now all my luck's upset, and ironically by the very person who gave me the charm in the first place.

With a stab of pain she recalled a pair of soft dark eyes and a tender kiss, one which could have been so different in different circumstances.

Suddenly she recalled that she still had the book that Martin Somerville had lent her, and his magnifying glass. Well, they could go back as soon as she could post them through the letterbox unseen. She never wanted that man back in her house again, end of story.

She glanced at the cat statuette as she straightened up, and could have sworn it had a smirk on its face. Childishly she stuck her tongue out at it.

'I said, the bread's getting low — shall I go down to the shop for a couple of extra loaves?'

'What? Oh, sorry, Mary, I was miles

away. Bread? Yes — oh, yes, please, if you would. Thanks.'

The other woman regarded her with concern. 'You've been doing that a lot lately, I've noticed. Daydreaming and suchlike. And you've been looking a bit whisht too, I thought.'

Helen smiled at the old Cornish word.

'Something up, is there?' Mary persisted. 'Got problems have you? Maybe it's none of my business, but sometimes it do help to talk things over. If you want to, that is.'

'Thanks, Mary, that's kind of you.' Helen gave her a smile of genuine gratitude. 'But I'm afraid that no-one can sort this out except me. But as soon as I can explain it all to you, I will, I promise.'

Mary nodded, and left for the shop.

Helen's eye caught sight of the letter from the planning officer which she had stuffed behind a plate on the kitchen dresser and hadn't looked at since. A bell rang in her head. Hadn't it said something about, if she wanted to appeal . . . get in touch with . . . some name or other? Maybe she would just do that. If she *was* going to have to give in, she could go down fighting at least.

With a determined stride she crossed the room and unfolded the letter. ' . . . *contact David Horrocks on* . . . ' and a phone number.

Her mouth set in a grim line, she went out to the hall and dialled the number given. Mr Horrocks was free on Thursday morning, said his secretary, should she arrange an appointment? Helen did so, wishing she didn't have to wait for three days. She was in a fighting mood now and didn't want it to wear off.

As she put the phone down her glance fell on the magnifying glass and book which she had placed on the hall table. She picked them up and went to the window. Good — there was no sign of movement from next door. She was on her way before she changed her mind.

With her heart hammering in her ribs she slid the book through the flap of the letterbox. For a heart-stopping moment she thought it might be too big, but with another shove it shot through with a clatter and landed on the floor inside. She hesitated with the glass. What if it cracked as it landed? And as she stood biting her lip in indecision, she heard footsteps approaching on the other side of the door.

Her heart was thumping so hard now that she wondered if he would hear it as the steps came nearer. Oh, goodness, what would she say? What would he say? Her legs were trembling. There was no way she could face him. She would just thrust the magnifying glass into his hand and run.

The door opened — and she was face to face with the elegant woman she had seen in the garden the other day. His wife! Blinded with fury, Helen hadn't anticipated this most obvious of events.

'Yes?' The woman's eyebrows rose and Helen realised how she must look to her: dishevelled, flushed, her face probably blotched from her recent tears — a mess, in fact.

'Oh. Is — is your husband at home?' Helen managed to stammer. 'I wanted to give him this.' She held out the glass.

The woman stared at her. 'My husband's in Dubai,' she replied. 'He won't be home for at least six months. Do you know him?' Her face was closed. 'I'm Elizabeth,' she added coolly. 'Can I help you at all?'

Dubai! What — ? How — ?

Helen gaped as the truth hit her. What had she done? She'd made a fool of herself! It had all been a huge mistake! Oh, how embarrassing! What could she say? And what had she said to him — to Martin? Such dreadful things!

She drew in a deep breath and blurted, 'Sorry, I meant . . . Martin — Martin Somerville. I — um — thought . . . '

'Oh, Martin!' Elizabeth's expression relaxed and she smiled faintly. 'Oh, you're mistaken. Martin's not my husband.'

'He's not?' said Helen faintly. 'Then what — who . . . ?'

'He's Jim's brother,' Elizabeth replied. 'He's been building this place for us while Jim's working abroad.'

'Oh I see,' said Helen in a small voice, as heat flooded her face. How could she have made such a monumental mistake? Jumping to conclusions like that! But she had seen them together. He was building the bungalow for this woman and her children and she had naturally assumed . . . She pulled herself together.

'I'm so sorry,' she said with as much dignity as she could muster. 'I made a silly mistake.' She was already backing away from the doorstep, ready to retreat.

Elizabeth's smile was warmer now. 'We're going to be neighbours in the near future,' she said, 'and I don't even know your name.'

Helen told her and they shook hands.

'We'll have to meet for coffee one day after we've moved in,' Elizabeth added.

'You can see what a mess I'm in still.' She gestured to the bags of cement lying in the hall behind her. 'I just called in to drop off some things before I take the children to school. I left the kids in the car for a minute.' She pointed towards the road where her car was parked. 'It's lucky you caught me. Shall I send Martin over when I see him next?' she asked. 'Or can I give him a message for you?'

'Um, no,' Helen said. 'No, thanks. Just give him this if you would — and the book there. He lent them to me, you see.'

'No problem. And I'll tell him you called,' Elizabeth replied. 'Nice to have met you,' she added, as Helen backed away.

'You too,' she said and withdrew, covering her confusion as well as she could.

What a fool she'd been! And she'd slapped his face! Mortified, Helen bit a nail to the quick as she relived the dreadful scene. She owed him an apology, didn't she? She was going to have to eat humble pie, crawl round there and explain that it had all been a misunderstanding . . .

She groaned and cringed inwardly at the very thought of it. It would be the hardest task she had ever faced in her life.

# The End Of A Dream

David Horrocks, the chief planning officer, was tall and wiry with a pleasant face and a quick smile, which did much to defuse Helen's initial antagonism. She had carefully rehearsed what she was going to say and was ready to fight her corner, but it all flew out of her head as he stood and held out his hand when she entered.

'Miss Matthews — good morning. Please sit down.'

He uttered some remark about the weather, then drew a folder towards him and pulled out some documents. Glancing at the top one he looked over his spectacles and said, 'Ah, yes, I have your file here. You applied to convert some land into a campsite, that was it, wasn't it?'

'Yes,' Helen replied. 'And apparently some rare plant has been found there which is going to prevent me from doing so.'

She leaned forward and looked him in the eye. 'Mr Horrocks, I *need* that land for my livelihood. I've just started running a holiday business and if I'm not able to expand I shan't be able to carry on. It's as simple as that.'

The man looked at her with sympathy and spread his hands. 'Believe me, I do understand your predicament, but it's not up to me and my committee alone. I'm powerless to change the decision because the area we are talking about has already been designated a Site of Special Scientific Interest. Not by us, but by a national body. Which means that our hands are tied while the area is being assessed.'

'And when did that happen?' Helen was on the edge of her seat, a frown on her face. 'That it was designated, I mean.'

David Horrocks riffled through his papers and eventually said, 'Three years ago, seemingly.'

'Three *years*?' Helen's eyes widened in astonishment. 'But that was long before the property came to me. Why wasn't I told?'

'Presumably because the previous owner had been informed, I should imagine.'

Helen gaped at him. 'Shouldn't it have been put on the deeds, or somewhere in writing?' she asked.

The man shrugged. 'There must have been a letter or a document of some kind at the time,' he replied. 'It has obviously been mislaid and not come down to you.'

That was quite likely, Helen was thinking, considering her aunt's age, her transfer from her home to residential care, and the chaotic state of her belongings which had been left behind. She calmed down a little. It didn't change the situation but it made it more understandable.

She bit her lip. There was still one thing which was puzzling her.

'Mr Horrocks,' she said, 'can you tell

me who it was that reported finding that fern? Is that in your records?'

'Um, let me see.' he turned a few pages. 'Ah yes.' He looked up at her. 'A Mr T. S. Matthews. Of the Nature Trust.' He smiled. 'Same name as you. That's a coincidence, isn't it?'

Tim? Her own brother! Helen's mouth dropped open with shock. He was the one who had dropped her in it — and he hadn't even had the decency to mention it to her! She mouthed a few platitudes, excused herself and ended the interview as quickly as she could.

Back home again, she furiously dialled her mother's number.

'Tim?' came Laura's voice. 'No, he's away — didn't you know? He's been in Wales for a fortnight on some project or other . . . No, I don't know how long he's staying for and no, I don't have a number for him. Sorry. You know your brother — he refuses to carry a mobile phone and the place where he's staying is somewhere inaccessible, halfway up a mountain, I think he said.'

She paused, then added in a measured tone, 'You seem to be a bit overwrought, dear. I suppose you're still working too hard. I did warn you . . . '

'Yes, Mum, I'm OK. Really. Must go. Bye.'

Helen slammed down the receiver before she could say something she'd regret later. Then, '*Men*,' she exploded. 'Who needs them?' First Alex, then Martin, and now Tim. She had been let down by them all. It hurt, and also left her feeling bereft and very much alone, with her hopes and dreams in tatters.

But wallowing in self-pity would get her nowhere. She set her mouth in a determined line. There was still work to be done.

It was now the middle of May. She had guests booked in at varying times from now until the end of September and would continue the business until then. Then she would sell up. If she was lucky, she might be able to sell the house reasonably quickly. Then she would bury the dream and pay off the worst of her debts. There would be nothing left of her savings by then and she would be forced to find a job and somewhere to live. And probably forced to leave Cornwall too.

★ ★ ★

A few days passed without incident until one morning when Helen went to answer the doorbell and found her brother on the step.

Her face flamed. 'Tim! At last. Have I got a bone to pick with you!'

'It's lovely to see you too,' he replied dryly, raising an eyebrow as she strode ahead of him down the passage and into the lounge.

Helen perched on the edge of an armchair and Tim slid into the one facing her.

'So, where's this bone you're talking about, then?' he said jauntily.

'Be serious for once, can't you?' Helen snapped. 'What do you mean by dropping me in it like that?' she demanded as he nonchalantly crossed one leg over the other and folded his arms across his chest.

'Yes, I had a good time in Wales, thanks for asking.' He regarded her levelly. 'Now calm down, for goodness' sake, and tell me what on earth you're so steamed up about, will you?'

'You mean, you really don't *know*?' Her mouth dropped open. 'That I've been refused permission to build on my field, all because of your precious Cretan *fern*?'

'First I've heard of it,' he replied.

'But the report had your name on it. I asked especially,' Helen stammered. 'How could you possibly not know?'

'You'd better tell me the whole story right from the beginning.'

Tim heard her out and when her voice trailed away and she came to a full stop, he uncrossed his legs and leaned towards her, resting both elbows on his knees.

'Right. Now hear my side of all this.

When I discovered that plant on your land I knew you were going to have problems. I didn't mention it to you at the time until I'd found out more details, but I went back to the Trust and sent in a report. I had to do that. My professional integrity would have been at stake if I'd just ignored it. You do understand that, don't you?'

'No,' she glowered, 'you're being pompous. But go on.'

He glared back at her but ignored the remark.

'Then I was unexpectedly sent up to Wales on this project, right out in the back of beyond, and as far as I was concerned the whole thing was shelved until I got back.' He shrugged and lifted his palms. 'It all took longer than it was meant to — and now you tell me that the planners have got hold of the report, is that it?'

'It certainly is,' Helen snapped. 'All my plans are ruined. In fact, my whole business is ruined, because without the campsite I'm not going to be able to make ends meet. Tim — ' she faced him and her shoulders slumped. ' — I'm going to have to sell up the whole place and forget it ever happened. It's that serious.' Her lips trembled. 'Now can you see why I didn't exactly welcome you with open arms?'

Tim nodded thoughtfully. 'I do see,' he said abstractedly. 'Look, sis, leave this with me and I'll see what I can do. I'll go into it all and find out what happened and how, and see if anything can be salvaged from it.'

'I can't imagine that you'll be able to change things now,' Helen retorted. 'It's far too late.'

'We'll see.' Tim slapped his hands on his knees and tried to lighten the mood by saying, 'So, yes, please, I'd love that cup of coffee you're just about to offer me.'

He gave her a wicked grin, and Helen couldn't help but smile back. At least Tim had explained his side of the story and had given her a faint ray of hope that it might not be all over yet. But she had too much sense to clutch at straws and wouldn't allow herself even to think about such a possibility.

Meanwhile, she was going to wring as much pleasure as she could out of the whole sorry mess. There was nothing so urgently waiting her attention that she couldn't leave it for an hour, and as soon as Tim had gone on his way she stepped outside into the sunshine and pulled the door shut behind her.

She took the cliff path which wound steeply up and over the top of the headland in the direction of Portreath, sniffing the salty air with appreciation. Far below her, surfers were skilfully riding the great breakers which were rolling in and smashing themselves on to the shore in curls of fretted white.

Perched almost on the edge of the cliff stood a roofless old engine-house, with tumbled stones nearby telling of the former tin and copper mining which had gone on years before. It must have been a perilous place in which to work, she thought, passing an old shaft which had been sunk frighteningly near the overhang, and noticing the adits which had been hewn into the cliff-face to drain the surplus water from its workings.

Great cushions of sea-pinks grew everywhere along the cliff-top and as she walked on Helen noticed that the turf at her feet was strewn with innumerable small wild flowers which glowed with jewel-bright colours. In places, groups of stately pyramid orchids thrust their vivid pink florets towards a sky of perfect cobalt blue.

Pyramids. Egypt. And what did that remind her of? She sat down on a granite boulder splattered with bright orange lichen and sighed deeply. She had managed to banish Martin Somerville to the back of her mind until now. But in all fairness she did owe him an apology and an explanation for her behaviour, in spite of what it was going to cost her in terms of pride.

She plucked a grass stem and nibbled on it, her eyes on the sparkling sea. She had put it off for long enough. It was time to square her conscience, bite the bullet, or whatever cliché fitted the situation, and seek him out.

★ ★ ★

She was thoughtful as she strolled homeward. She would have to find out where he lived and call on him. It was no use waiting for him to appear next door. She had prevaricated for long enough. But how — ? Ah — Ruth Taylor would know. Hadn't she once said that Martin was lodging with a relative of hers, or something?

And there was Ruth now. As Helen walked down the hill she could see the woman cutting the grass in her small front garden, and could hear the hum of the hover-mower.

Helen crossed the road and leaned over the wall until Ruth noticed her and cut the engine of the mower.

'Hello, my 'andsome, haven't seen you for some long time,' she said with a smile, wiping the back of her hand across her forehead. 'Phew! Hot work this is.' Helen grinned, for Ruth was wearing a print dress with a cardigan over it, and her plump legs were sheathed in thick tights. 'Some lovely day though, isn't it?' she added.

'Yes, it's glorious,' Helen agreed. 'I've just been up on the cliffs for a walk and it's feeling really like summer.'

The formalities over, Helen brought up the subject of her visit. 'I was wondering if you can tell me where Martin Somerville lives. I need to see him about something. Didn't you say once that he lodges with one of your relations?'

'Oh, well, not exactly. But he do rent a cottage what belong to my cousin Henry, that's what. Up Stippy-Stappy 'tis. Can't remember the number, but anyone'll tell you when you get there.'

'Oh, right.' Helen smiled at the quaint but accurate name of the terrace, which descended the hillside in a series of steps, each cottage being slightly lower than its neighbour, the whole thing looking from above just like a staircase.

They chatted then over a few trivialities before Helen moved on. She firmly resisted the temptation to turn in at her own drive. If she went home now she would chicken out of his visit, and there was no excuse to put it off any longer.

Taking a deep breath, she started up the road to Stippy-Stappy.

The slope where the cottages were situated was wooded and the trees in full new leaf were ringing with bird-song. A stream fringed with ferns and cresses gurgled happily on its way to the sea, and at any other time she would have enjoyed the walk. But her head was full of only one thing as she marched up the hill: whether Martin would be in and what his reaction would be at the sight of her. She glanced at her watch. It was mid-day and she was banking on him coming home for his lunch. Even if she had to hang about and wait for a while, she told herself that she wasn't budging until she'd spoken to him.

* * *

She reached the row of cottages and was looking about for someone who might tell her where he lived, when her heart missed a beat and her mouth went suddenly dry. There was no need to enquire after all, for there was Martin, just going in through his gate. And he'd seen her. She could tell that by the almost imperceptible start he gave before he continued on his way, marching purposefully up to the front door.

Before he had a chance to close it against her, she was behind him and calling his name. 'Martin — please — can I have a word with you?'

He turned to her and his expression was as unyielding as a granite rock. 'Oh, it's you.' His voice was like ice-water running over the rock. 'I can't imagine that we have anything whatsoever to say to each other,' he replied.

His face was closed and his eyes like twin black pebbles as they bored into hers. Helen swallowed. This was going to be even worse than she'd thought.

She ploughed on, her face as pink as the shirt she wore. 'I — I need to talk to you. Privately,' she added as she became aware of curious stares from several of his neighbours who were chatting in a little knot together over somebody's gate. 'Please, Martin — can I come in for a moment?'

Following the direction of her glance, he grunted. 'I suppose so, if you must.'

He stood back and let her precede him into the hall, where he jerked his head towards an open door on the right and added, 'In there,' as he dumped his briefcase on the hall floor and hung his jacket on a peg beside it.

Helen sank into a deep armchair, glad to rest her shaking legs, and Martin faced her from another. She could hear a radio playing in the house next door, and a blackbird was singing in the sycamore tree outside the window. To the rest of the village it was just an ordinary day.

'I've only come home for a quick lunch,' Martin said briskly, glancing at the carriage clock on the mantelpiece. 'I've got an appointment in an hour.'

He was wearing a white shirt with a striped tie and the trousers of his business suit. It was the first time she had seen him so formally dressed and it made him look even more formidable.

She swallowed again and took a deep breath.

'It — it won't take very long.' She fixed her gaze on her clasped hands in her lap. 'I've come because — because, you see, I owe you an apology.'

'Oh, yes?' The relentless stare continued. So he wasn't going to make it easy for her, she thought.

She lifted her chin and her eyes locked with his. 'Martin, I made a terrible mistake. Two, in fact,' she blurted. 'When I had the letter from the council I jumped to the conclusion that it must have been you who had told them about the fern, because I thought you were the only person to have been up to the field.'

She gulped and twisted her fingers in her lap as she tore her gaze away from that implacable face.

'But I was wrong — and I know that now. So I'm sorry that I bawled you out that day, but I hope you can understand why, now that I've explained it.'

A silence fell, and she raised her head. Was she imagining it, or was there a hint of softening in that stony stare?

'I see,' came the terse reply. No, she'd been wrong. He seemed to be actually enjoying her humiliation, and she could have kicked him.

'Go on,' he snapped, as straight-faced as ever. 'You said there was something else.'

Now for the part she had been dreading most of all. She felt her cheeks burning and there was no way she could meet his eyes any more. Her stomach was churning and she felt sick.

She licked dry lips and blurted, 'The other thing was a silly misunderstanding on my part. You see, I thought you were . . . that you were married. To Elizabeth . . . and that was why I called you names when . . .'

Her voice trailed away. There — she'd done it. She had told him everything. She had bared her soul and had nothing more to give. She sank her face in her hands as hot tears seared her eyelids and began to squeeze through her clenched fingers.

Then she heard a strange noise. It sounded like a snort. Or a chuckle. Then came a full-scale burst of laughter.

It was so surprising that her tears dried in an instant as she raised her eyes. To her utter astonishment Martin had thrown back his head and was shaking with laughter, great guffaws which filled the room and had him wiping his eyes as he struggled to speak.

When he finally managed to control himself he leaned forward in his chair and spluttered, 'Me? Married to *Elizabeth*! Whatever gave you that idea?'

'Well, what's so funny about it?' Helen retorted, riled now. 'You were building her a bungalow — I saw you over there together — how was I to know that it wasn't for you as well? And I heard someone call her Mrs Somerville. Besides, Ruth Taylor thought so too, and she told me . . .'

'Well, let's just say that's what comes of listening to village gossip too much.' Martin's eyes were still twinkling with humour and all of a sudden Helen found herself smiling back. She could feel the tension flowing out of her. It was replaced by an indescribable relief as the realisation that it was going to be all right filled her.

'No,' Martin went on. 'I'm single — now.' He paused and Helen pondered the significance of that 'now'. But before she had a chance to take it in properly, he went on, 'And I shouldn't have taken the liberty I did. It's my turn to apologise to you.' His voice was formal, with no trace of the amusement of only a moment ago.

Helen wanted to tell him that no apology was needed, for she recalled how her body had reacted to his kiss. But what could she say, how could she put it?

While she was still struggling for the words, Martin went on, 'Thanks for coming round, I appreciate it.' With a perception that surprised her he finished, 'It can't have been easy for you.'

He regarded her with a level stare until she lowered her eyes and murmured, 'No.'

There was a short silence between them, during which the blackbird continued his song of happiness outside the window.

'No hard feelings then?' she asked as she glanced up into his face again.

'Oh no, none. Let's draw a line under the whole thing and pretend none of it ever happened, shall we?' His voice was gentle as their eyes locked.

There was a pause, until Martin

suddenly stood up. 'Right. And just to prove there's no ill-feeling, how about some lunch?' he said briskly, looking down at her and this time his face was open and friendly.

'But,' Helen began, 'You're in a hurry, aren't you? You said you have an appointment . . . '

'Ah.' He looked shame-faced. 'That was my fall-back when I didn't know how this meeting was going to turn out.' He grinned again. 'It's actually a dental appointment, but not until four o'clock. I was a bit economical with the truth there. Sorry! How about letting me make amends with a tuna sandwich? That suit you?'

'Fine.' Helen was scarcely taking in what she was hearing. 'Let me help.'

Martin moved towards the door and said, 'Right. The kitchen's this way.'

Helen could hardly believe this was happening. After all the time it had taken for her to work up enough courage to face this man, the air had been cleared in about ten minutes and now here they were, preparing a meal together like the best of friends. She almost had to pinch herself to prove that it was no dream.

★　★　★

'Now, to go back to what you were saying when you first came in,' Martin said when they were comfortably seated at the kitchen breakfast bar. 'It hasn't occurred to you, has it, that if *you've* been refused planning permission to build on your land, then *I'll* get the same treatment, since the fields are adjacent to each other?'

He speared a slice of tomato with his fork, regarded her calmly over the fork and popped the tomato into his mouth.

Helen almost choked on a bite of her sandwich as realisation hit her.

'Oh, Martin — no, I didn't!' She looked at him in consternation. 'So of course it couldn't have been you who made the report. Oh, what a fool I've been! I'm really sorry. Can you ever forgive me?'

He leaned across and patted her hand. 'There's nothing to forgive. Naturally you were too upset to think about anything but your own problems.'

He sighed and gazed out of the window at the lush greenery of the trees. 'But I shall have to give up my dream as well. I was hoping to live up there myself, you see.'

Helen nodded as his eyes met hers. He hadn't removed the hand and was holding her gaze until she felt almost mesmerised. Close to — and they were very close across the narrow breakfast bar — she could see little gold flecks dancing in the shining depths of his eyes. They were a rich bitter-chocolate brown, she noted. And he was no rat after all — quite the reverse, in fact.

She smiled and nodded in sympathy as she felt her spirits give a little lift.

'More salad?' Martin asked prosaically, withdrawing the hand as he turned back to his lunch. And as he moved, a ray of sunshine glanced off the ring he was wearing. It looked like a wedding band, Helen noted, but he was wearing it on his right hand.

'Oh, um — no, thank you,' she replied, coming back to earth. 'That was fine. That sandwich was delicious. Do you live alone?' she asked, fishing.

He nodded. 'Mary comes in to clean once a week,' he replied.

Helen raised an eyebrow. 'Mary Harris?' she said and he nodded. 'She's never mentioned it to me.'

Martin shrugged. 'Just an oversight, I suppose.' He pushed his plate to one side. 'But other than that I look after myself,' he went on. 'I'm not a bad cook, of the freezer-to-microwave type,' he added with a grin.

Then the smile faded as he muttered under his breath something that Helen didn't quite catch, but which sounded liked, 'I was married — once . . . ' and his eyes were suddenly bleak.

Helen waited to see if he was going to enlarge on this, but a silence fell and he seemed lost in thoughts of his own. Eventually he came back from whatever dark place he had visited and asked, 'What about you? Are you single?' She felt sure it was an effort to deflect the conversation from himself.

She nodded. 'Yes. There was someone, in London, but . . . ' She shrugged, not prepared to go into detail.

To relieve the tension which appeared to be deepening, she, too, changed the subject.

'You haven't heard from the planning committee yet, I suppose?' she asked, stirring her coffee reflectively.

'No, but I'm sure I shall before long. At least now that I know the outcome, it won't be quite such a shock.'

'I went to see if I could appeal against it,' Helen went on, 'but not a chance.'

A small silence fell between them again as they both pondered on their vanished hopes.

'Oh, I know what I almost forgot to tell you,' said Helen, breaking the silence.

Martin's brows rose enquiringly. 'When my mother came round the other day, she told me that Grace once had a lovely garden up behind the house, at the bottom of that field. With statues and things that she'd brought back from her travels. So I went to have a good look and you'll never guess what I found!' She paused for effect. Then, 'A model of the Sphinx,' she said, and waited for his reaction.

She wasn't disappointed. His eyes widened and his whole face lit up with interest. 'Really?' he said. 'Was there anything else?'

She shook her head. 'There are one or two lumps and bumps in the grass,' she replied, 'but nothing I can easily move on my own.'

'It sounds exciting,' Martin said. 'A bit like a treasure hunt. I'll come over and have a look at that statue. Then between us we might manage to unearth some other stuff.'

'OK,' Helen replied, smiling to herself. It was typical of him not to wait to be invited! But she no longer seemed to mind.

'I'll come as soon as I get back from the dentist,' he said. 'OK?'

'Fine,' Helen agreed with a nod. 'Now, I must go. Thanks for lunch.'

He rose to see her to the door. 'You're very welcome,' he replied. 'Thank you again for coming.'

He looked deeply into her eyes as seconds ticked by, until Helen tore herself away and started down the steps.

'I'll see you later,' she called back over her shoulder.

Martin raised a hand and watched her until she was out of sight.

★　★　★

Helen was ready with fork and spade by the time Martin returned. But as she opened the door to his knock, he gave her such a lop-sided grin that it sent her into peals of laughter.

'I know, I know,' he groaned, holding

a hand to his cheek as he came in.

'Let me guess,' Helen said. 'A filling?'

He nodded. 'At the back. The dentist had quite a job getting at it and it took ages. At least it didn't hurt too badly. It's just that the after-effects take so long to wear off, don't they?'

'Poor you,' said Helen. 'Well, there's no point in offering you a coffee just now, is there?'

'No, thanks — I wouldn't be able to manage it without a bib!' He grinned. 'We might as well get on with the grand search of the garden.'

He'd dressed down into jeans and a yellow short-sleeved polo shirt and was carrying a pair of muddy boots in one hand.

'I'll put these on outside,' he said, walking through the house to sit on the back doorstep and take off his trainers.

'I don't think I'll risk those wellies again after what happened last time,' said Helen, then reddened as she realised what she'd said. She had meant her fall, of course, but too late she remembered what had followed the fall!

'Here you are,' she said, thrusting a spade at him as he rose to his feet, and then led the way purposefully up to the field to hide her flaming cheeks.

By the time Martin had caught her up, the light breeze off the sea had cooled Helen's face. She stopped beside the statue of the Sphinx and pointed. 'There,' she said. 'I gave it a scrub the other day and it's come up really well.'

'Oh . . . yes . . . I should say so.' He drew closer and bent down to peer at the figure. 'It's perfect — not a chip or a scratch. Amazing.' He paused with his hand on the Sphinx's head and looked around. 'I wonder if there's anything else?'

'I had a look at this stone over here in the grass,' Helen replied, taking a few steps to the side. 'It seems to be made of the same kind of material as the statue. What do you think?'

'Let's see . . . ' Martin lifted his fork, inserted it underneath the stone and put his weight on it. 'You do the same

186

on the other side,' he instructed, and Helen jabbed her spade in the soil. 'Now we'll try to turn it over,' he decided. 'Both together — heave — that's it — oh, brilliant!' he exclaimed as the great stone moved, rose and toppled just as he had indicated.

'Wow! It *is* something!' Helen exclaimed, bending over it and brushing off some of the clinging soil with her fingers. The ground was dry, there had been no rain for a while and the crumbly dirt came away fairly easily.

Martin watched intently as she roughly cleaned it up then rose to her feet to take a look at the whole thing. 'It's a god or something,' she said, wiping her hands on her trousers. 'Give me a hand to lift it up.'

Once it was upright, they stepped back a pace for a better view.

'It *is* a god, I think — it looks like a human figure,' said Helen as she peered at the object.

'Well, semi-human anyway,' Martin

amended. Seated on a throne, the body of the statue was that of a nubile young woman, but her head was that of a cat. Crowned with her identifying sacred head-dress, she was exactly like the little model Martin had given Helen.

'It's Bast!' they both exclaimed together, and turned to each other in delight.

'All we need now is to find a model of Horus to make the pair,' Helen laughed as they turned over several more stones.

Some were just what they looked like — rubble — and although by the end of the day they had unearthed a small pyramid and two more statues, nothing resembled the falcon-headed god.

'We'll have to look this pair up in the book,' Martin said, straightening and pressing one hand to his weary back.

Helen leaned on the handle of her fork and looked up and down the field. 'I think that's it,' she said. 'I can't see any more likely looking stones, can you?'

'No,' he replied, 'and if there were, they would have to wait until tomorrow — my back's killing me!'

'Are you all right?' Helen asked with concern. 'You would do all the heavy lifting yourself. I could have helped more if you'd let me.'

'It's nothing a hot bath won't cure.' He hefted his spade across his shoulder and added with a grin, 'And I can't help being a perfect gentleman, you know. It comes with the image.'

'Oh, you . . . ' She grinned, thinking what a great step forward their relationship had taken, that they were now so easy in each other's company.

As they walked back to the house together, Martin glanced at her. 'What are you going to do with all your statuary? Have you thought?'

'It did cross my mind that sometime in the future I might restore Aunt Grace's garden,' she replied. 'But that was before. Now it looks like I'll have to abandon my plans for the campsite, and it's also glaringly obvious that without it

I shan't be able to keep up the business, so — ' She turned to him and added bleakly, 'So I guess they'll have to stay just where they are and get lost in the undergrowth again for someone else to find after I've sold up.'

# Big Surprises!

Helen awoke a couple of days later to the realisation that it was her twenty-seventh birthday — and the first one in her life that she had ever spent on her own.

It wasn't an auspicious start to what should have been a happy occasion, but as she picked up the post from the mat she resolved to enjoy it as best she could. She had a day with next to no commitments, and could please herself as to how she spent it. Not that she had the least idea of what she wanted to do!

She took the handful of cards into the kitchen and opened them as she ate her toast. There were no surprises, but at least no-one had forgotten her.

She was clearing up the kitchen and wondering how best to spend the day, when, surprisingly, the doorbell rang. She wasn't expecting any visitors.

A florist's van had pulled up in the drive and the delivery man was standing on the doorstep with his arms full of flowers. Helen's jaw dropped, then her face lit up with delight as he handed them over. 'Happy birthday, miss,' he said with a broad grin. 'These are for you.'

She thanked him and returned inside, scrabbling for the card that went with the bouquet. Who on earth could have sent them?

' *'From the sun god to the goddess of the moon'*,' she read. ''*Many happy returns. Will see you later. Lunch? Horus.*' '

'Idiot!' she said with a giggle. But how had he known it was her birthday? And he was coming over! 'Lunch.' Did he mean he was taking her out to lunch?

She gave a little skip of excitement and her eyes were shining as she fetched a vase and some water and began to arrange the gorgeous blooms. There were lilies, great white-trumpeted lilies with golden hearts and a scent straight out of heaven. These were complemented by wide-eyed, brilliantly-coloured gerberas and fat pink roses in the full flush of perfection.

Helen buried her face in them, dizzy with joy and with their heady fragrance.

Then she raced upstairs to shower and change into something suitable for a lunch date.

From the wardrobe she pulled out a pair of smart cotton trousers and a sea-green top that she knew matched the colour of her eyes, because Alex had once told her so.

Alex. She paused for a moment with the garment in her hand and gazed out of the window. Strange, she thought — after how upset she'd been at their break-up, she hardly ever thought of him at all now.

As she threaded a pair of tiny silver stars through her ears and rolled on some mascara, it occurred to her that she had scarcely bothered with her appearance since coming back to

Cornwall. It hadn't seemed to matter when she was kept so busy with the house, and she hadn't been farther than Truro for essential shopping since she'd moved in. Her life had shrunk down to a very narrow radius — not that she felt there was anything wrong with that. It had been just as she'd wanted it to be, until now, of course . . .

She thrust these gloomy thoughts away, determined that, at least for today, she wouldn't dwell on her troubles.

She brushed her hair until it shone, dabbed on a hint of perfume and ran downstairs just in time to answer the door for the second time that morning.

This time it was Martin who was standing there, dressed in smart navy chinos and a soft wool sweater in shades of blue and grey.

'Happy birthday,' he said with a grin as she stood back to let him in, and he dropped a peck of a kiss on her cheek.

'The flowers are absolutely lovely,' she said as she led him through into the lounge. 'Thank you so much.' She stroked the perfect petal of one of the lilies as she spoke and bent her head to sniff its fragrance.

'Glad you like them,' he replied. 'I thought we might go out to lunch — if you'd like to, that is.' He looked down and scuffed a toe in the carpet.

He's actually looking self-conscious, Helen thought wonderingly; a bit unsure of himself. It was something she had never seen in him before — he was usually so self-assured.

Martin raised his head and met her eyes. His own were dancing with amusement now. 'I thought we could rise to something a bit more inspiring than a tuna sandwich, in honour of the occasion.'

Helen smiled back. 'I'd love to,' she said, 'but there's nothing wrong with a tuna sandwich in the right circum-stances!'

He laughed in agreement.

Martin drove through Truro and on to the Malpas Road that wended its way beside the River Fal, where pleasure boats rocked at their moorings and water fowl foraged among the mudflats exposed by the ebb-tide.

A wave of contentment washed over Helen. This was certainly a lovely part of the country and she was glad to be spending her birthday here, with this man.

⋆　⋆　⋆

They ate lunch in an attractive riverside pub where it was sheltered enough to sit outside and enjoy the view. The late May sunshine streamed down and set every ripple sparkling, and on the other side of the water, dense woodland sloped down to the edge, its foliage brilliant in shades of new green.

As Helen watched, a heron flapped its way lazily up-stream where its mate was standing on stilt-like legs, head hunched into its neck, patiently waiting for a catch.

'What a fantastic spot,' she said,

leaning back in her chair and tipping her face up to the sun. 'It's almost warm enough to get a tan.'

'It's always more sheltered on the south coast,' Martin replied. 'Very different from where we live. Our wind comes straight across the Atlantic with nothing to stop it between us and America!'

He slid back his chair and stretched out his long legs, then leant back with both arms behind his head. 'That was really good,' he said with a contented sigh. 'I haven't eaten this well in ages.'

'It certainly has to be better than your freezer-to-microwave style,' she agreed, pushing back her cleared plate. 'It *was* delicious.'

Martin had closed his eyes against the sun and Helen took the opportunity to study his face. Relaxed, he looked younger than she reckoned he must be, and the air of self-importance which he normally wore had disappeared, replaced now by a softer expression entirely, and one which was far more attractive.

She recalled the first time they had met, when she had just arrived at the house. What an arrogant individual she'd thought him. How wrong she had been.

Since then, their relationship had been so fraught with misunderstandings that she realised she'd never known the real person. But now she was very much aware of him, and also of her own altered feelings.

In this beautiful place she could forget all the worries waiting for her at home, relax and let her real self surface. And at last she forced herself to admit that she was attracted to this man. She had been for ages really, but she had never realised that the strong feelings he aroused in her were not anger or irritation or any of the negatives, but something much deeper and more positive.

Lost in her reverie, she didn't notice that he'd opened his eyes and was staring straight at her. She jumped and felt colour rise to her cheeks. Wordlessly he reached his hand across the table and caught hers in a warm clasp, drawing her to her feet.

'How about a walk to work off all that food?'

She forced herself out of the dream. 'Great idea,' she agreed.

'I can see a track along by the river down there. Let's see where it goes, shall we?' he said, still holding her hand.

The path led them along the edge of the creek, over shingle and stones which were green with algae and seaweed, for the tide was out. Scrubby oaks bent low over the shore, hanging almost horizontally in places, as their exposed and gnarled roots struggled to keep their grip in the eroded soil. Clumps of dry seaweed had been blown into their lower branches and were waving in the breeze like some new variety of foliage.

Over a stile and the track began to climb upwards, skirting a field and emerging into a conifer wood. Here the sun was veiled by the branches of the tall pines and the two were walking on a springy carpet of fallen needles, the resinous scent rising in the warm air like incense. Framed by the trees, the water was intensely blue and they stopped for a moment to watch a couple of cormorants standing on a fallen log, their lustrous black wings outstretched to dry in the sun.

'This path seems to go on for ever,' Helen remarked after they had been walking for half an hour. 'Perhaps we should turn back.' She had put on a pair of smart shoes for their lunch date, which were quite unsuitable for this terrain, and was wishing now that she'd stuck to her trainers.

'You're right,' said Martin. 'I was hoping there might be a circular route, but without a map I could be wrong. We'll go back the way we came.'

They eventually arrived back at the stile, which was much steeper from this side. Martin climbed over first, then held out a hand to help Helen, who was teetering on the top step as her wretched shoes slipped on the damp stone.

'Steady now, I've got you.' Seeing her predicament, he put both hands to her waist and lifted her over. 'OK?' he asked with concern, and Helen nodded, her face very close to his.

Martin seemed in no hurry to release her and they regarded each other for a long minute. It was so quiet that she heard a fish pop to the surface of the water, while in the bushes nearby a blackbird was singing its heart out, not a bit disturbed by their presence.

Helen swayed towards him and closed her eyes against the sun, as she waited for what must surely come. But he stepped briskly away from her and said, 'Good,' before turning his back on her and leading the way down the remainder of the narrow path towards the car.

Helen followed mutely, stunned and disappointed.

They drove home in virtual silence, broken only by a few pleasantries, each seemingly deep in thoughts of their own.

When Martin pulled up outside her house, Helen turned to him and said with sincerity, 'That was wonderful, thanks for everything. I've had a lovely birthday — much better than I'd expected.' She opened the car door and began to climb out, but then glanced back. 'Would you like to come in for a drink?' she asked.

He consulted his watch and shook his head. 'Thanks, but no thanks. I have to go away for a while on a business matter, and I'm leaving in the morning. I must put a few things together and sort myself out before then.' He added, 'I enjoyed today, too. I'll see you when I get back.'

As she trudged up the path to her front door, feeling as if a shadow had come across the sun to spoil the end of her lovely day, he gave a wave and a smile and drove away.

★   ★   ★

A week later, Helen was out in the garden pulling up the weeds which had been sprouting rapidly owing to the warm, moist weather of the past few days.

She had neither seen nor heard anything from Martin since her birthday and was feeling low-spirited and edgy. After that lovely day, she had thought they might be entering a new stage in their relationship. But apparently not. Yes, he had said he was going away for a few days, but there was such a thing as a telephone, for goodness' sake! Just a brief call would have made all the difference.

She sighed. Had she said something that he could have taken the wrong way, she wondered, thinking back to his coolness when they had parted. But rack her brains as she might, she couldn't think of anything.

The only other explanation was, of course, that he had decided he didn't want them to get any closer, and he was backing off, hoping that she would take the hint. If that was it, there was nothing she could do about it.

Suddenly a cheery voice hailed her from behind and she jumped, startled, and turned to see two official-looking men in hard hats and yellow dayglo jackets who had opened the gate and were coming towards her. One was carrying a camera and tripod, the other had a clipboard under his arm and a document case slung over one shoulder.

Helen straightened up as they advanced, and wiped the soil from her hands down the sides of her dirty old jeans.

'Good morning. Would you be Miss Matthews?' The smile was friendly and open and Helen nodded. 'We're from English Heritage and the district council. I'm Mike and this is Bob. We've been sent to do a survey of the area and we need permission to cross your land.'

Helen's eyes widened. 'Oh, yes? What sort of survey?'

'It's to do with the old mining remains,' the man called Mike went on. 'We have to get close enough to the site to have a look round and see what there actually is up there. As you may or may not know, there's a scheme currently underway to preserve some of the more important of the industrial relics.'

Helen shook her head. 'No, no, I hadn't heard anything about it.'

Her brain had begun working overtime. Was this Tim's doing or was it sheer coincidence? What exactly were the authorities going to do and was it going to make any difference to her own position?

'So, would you mind if we just take a walk up there?' the other man, Bob, put in. 'It won't take long and we'll be careful not to disturb anything.'

'Feel free to go where you like,' Helen replied with a smile. 'There's nothing up there to disturb but a few goats.' And a protected plant, which she had no intention of mentioning. If it got trampled to death under their heavy work-boots, so much the better, she thought grimly.

'Fine. Thanks a lot.'

They went around the side of the house and up towards the field as Helen looked thoughtfully after them.

She picked up her tools and went indoors to wash and tidy herself, still thinking about what the man — Mike? — had said. Now that he had jogged her memory, she did recall reading in the local paper, ages ago now, about a couple of engine-houses somewhere — Camborne? Redruth? — that had been conserved in some way. There had been a photograph, and a big spread about a ceremony to launch the scheme. That must be what he meant. Hmm, interesting.

She was standing at the kitchen window later, washing dishes at the sink, when the two men walked past and called out their thanks before disappearing down the road with a smile and a wave.

★ ★ ★

Later, Helen was relaxing on the sofa, glad of a rest after all her gardening. She had a cup of tea at her elbow and was sipping it as she scanned the local paper. Glancing up, she caught sight of the Eye of Horus regarding her solemnly from its niche in the window.

Feeling restless, she let the paper drop to the floor as she rose to her feet and paced up and down the room. She couldn't get Martin out of her mind. His infectious grin and twinkling eyes intruded on every move she made, and echoes of their conversations played over and over inside her head.

Where was he? And just what — if anything — was there between them now?

Exasperated, she trudged upstairs to check the summer bookings on her computer. She couldn't let things like that slide. She had a business to run, for a few months more at least, she thought sadly.

Some days later she was working on her computer, checking on another booking, when she became aware of the sound of a child's piping voice outside. Assuming that Elizabeth and her family were visiting their nearly-completed bungalow, she thought no more about it until a ring came at her own front door.

She ran downstairs, annoyed at the interruption — and there he was. Martin. He was standing on the doorstep, and in his arms he was carrying a little girl.

'Hi, Helen. All right?' he said, as she looked at him with surprise. There was an expression on his face that she would have described almost as nervous, had she not known him so well.

With great self-control she managed not to return his smile, but said coolly, 'Yes, fine,' as she opened the door more widely, expecting him to walk in as usual.

However, he hesitated on the step

and cleared his throat. Then, 'Can I come in for a minute? If you're not busy, that is,' he asked.

Helen looked at him in astonishment. He was never this reticent — and he certainly never waited for an invitation!

'Of course.'

She led the way into the lounge and they sat down.

'Who's your little friend?' she asked, smiling at the child, who looked to be about two or three years old and was clutching a teddy bear in one hand. 'Babysitting for Elizabeth, are you?'

Martin sank into a chair and the little girl curled into his shoulder, her thumb in her mouth as she stared at Helen with large, dark eyes.

'Um — no, not exactly,' he said, avoiding Helen's eyes. 'She's not Elizabeth's. That's what I've come to talk to you about. You see, this is Clare. My daughter.'

'*Your* daughter?' Helen's eyebrows rose to her hairline with astonishment. 'B — but — you never mentioned

. . . why didn't you tell me before?'

Martin looked down at the top of the child's head and went on, 'Because until now I wasn't sure about our feelings for each other, Helen. And, of course, I'm still not sure how you feel about me. But for my part,' he ploughed on, and Helen realised with sudden sympathy how difficult this must be for him, 'ever since your birthday I haven't stopped thinking about you, and what a great deal you've come to mean to me.'

He raised his head to look into her face, and Helen felt a wave of joy surge through her. It was going to be all right after all. All her doubts and fears had been for nothing.

As she smiled at him, she knew that her heart was in her eyes.

She was about to speak when he winced suddenly as, with a gurgle of amusement, his daughter grabbed hold of a lock of his hair and tugged.

'Ouch!' he said as he unhooked himself.

The incident changed the whole highly-charged situation and Helen joined in the fun as they all laughed together.

'So you see,' Martin raised his head again and met her eyes, 'I had to come and tell you the truth and bring Clare along, so that you'll know everything there is to know before we go any farther in our relationship — if you want to, that is . . . ' He came to a stumbling halt and a small silence fell between them.

Impulsively Helen went to kneel beside his chair. 'Martin, of course I do,' she said. 'You don't know . . . these past weeks . . . how I — how I've missed you,' she said, looking at the child to avoid his gaze.

She took the small hand in hers. 'And your little girl is beautiful,' she went on.

Clare didn't pull away and Helen stroked the teddy bear's head with her other hand. 'Who's this, then?' she asked gently. 'Is he Winnie The Pooh?'

she added as she noticed the red jacket it was wearing.

Clare removed the thumb from her mouth and sat up straighter. 'Pooh,' she echoed, hugging the toy, and added, 'Tigger and Piglet home.'

'You've got Tigger and Piglet too? Lucky you,' Helen replied. 'Will you bring them to see me one day?'

The little girl nodded solemnly, her eyes never leaving Helen's face.

Helen looked up at Martin. 'She's so like you,' she said. 'It's amazing. But . . . your wife ..?' She stumbled over the question. But he had said he *had* been married — *once* — hadn't he? As if it were all over . . .

'Jennifer died giving birth to this little one,' he said simply, his eyes full of pain and Helen's heart went out to him. 'That was two and a half years ago. It was a difficult birth and there was internal bleeding.' He raised his shoulders in a gesture of hopelessness. 'So you see, Clare has never had a mother.'

Helen gripped his hand with sympathy. 'Oh, Martin, I'm so sorry — so terribly sorry.' Words could never be enough, she thought, but what else was there when faced with such tragedy?

'Thanks. I wanted you to know everything,' he added.

'I can't imagine how you got through such a traumatic time,' she said. 'And how do you manage now? With Clare, I mean?'

'Jennifer's parents are marvellous,' he replied. 'What I would have done without them I don't know. Especially her mother. She's been a tower of strength all along.'

He paused reflectively, then went on, 'They live not far from here and I moved in with the baby at first, and sold my own home. I couldn't bear the memories, you see.' He rasped a hand across his jaw and took a deep breath.

'But theirs is only a tiny cottage and there wasn't really room for all of us and the baby stuff too. So I moved into the rented place at Stippy-Stappy until

213

I could decide what to do. I couldn't possibly look after a baby on my own and continue to work, so I left Clare with Sylvia — Jennifer's mother — and I spend as much time with her as I can.'

Helen was transfixed by the whole story. What he had been through — and she had thought him arrogant and self-centred, when all the time — oh, how wrong she had been!

Martin was still talking. It was as if, having kept silent for so long, it was all spilling out now like a flood tide.

'Now that Clare's getting older and is past the real baby stage, I can cope better with her.

'And that's one reason I wanted to buy your land,' he went on. 'I was aiming to build a few bungalows, one of which was to have been for all of us. I'd planned to divide it so that we could all have our privacy, yet Sylvia could still look after Clare when I was at work.'

Helen's eyes widened. Now she could see why he'd been so eager for her to sell up. And she had thought him so ruthless and money-grabbing! She winced as she recalled how antagonistic she'd been, and wished they could go back and start all over again.

'So what are you going to do now that it's fallen through?' she wondered.

'I've managed to find another site,' Martin replied. 'That's what I've been doing these last few days: negotiating a tricky deal. It was far too highly-priced at first. But it's worked out OK and I've bought a plot of land — which has already been granted permission for building. And even better news, it's big enough for two separate dwellings, with easy access between them. I can be living really close by, but each of us will have our own home.' His face was animated now, his eyes lively.

'Fantastic. I'm really pleased for you,' said Helen sincerely.

She was rising to her feet when Martin put out a hand to detain her.

'Helen,' he said, looking into her face, 'I know it's early days yet, but when — that is, after I've got everything sorted — well, do you think . . . that we might consider a future together?'

For a long moment they were still, eyes locked, acutely aware of each other and of this pivotal moment in their lives. Then Helen nodded, her heart overflowing with joy, and Martin bent forward to place a soft kiss on her lips. Squashed between them, Clare gave an indignant wail and the precious moment was abruptly ended.

Martin looked so crestfallen that Helen squeezed his arm and whispered, 'It doesn't matter. Now that we're sure of each other, there'll be plenty of time for us later on. The whole of the rest of our lives, in fact.'

'Oh, Helen, you've made me so happy — and so relieved.' He looked close to breaking point, and Helen grasped his hand and held it to her cheek. 'I was dreading this meeting, dreading that you wouldn't want anything more to do with me when you knew . . . '

'And I thought — when you stayed away so long, that I'd said something to upset you!' Her laugh turned into a sob and she swallowed hard.

'Coffee,' she said firmly, deliberately defusing the tension. Releasing his hand with a gentle pat she laid it in his lap. 'That's what we both need — a dose of caffeine-rich, sugar-laced, totally wicked coffee! And some juice for Clare, of course.'

The last signs of strain on Martin's face eased, and he and the little girl followed her into the kitchen. Helen's glance met the staring Eye of Horus, and with a broad grin she gave it a mental 'thumbs-up'. Superstition or not, the charm had certainly worked for her.

'We'll talk soon,' Martin said later as he turned to go. 'Shall I come round tomorrow afternoon?'

Helen nodded and as she closed the door behind them she thought with a surge of excitement that the future wasn't looking so bleak now after all.

Martin loved her! And why had she been dragging her feet for so long, unwilling to admit that this was what she had been feeling about him almost from the beginning?

She just hadn't recognised it for what it was. She'd thought she hated him, because of what she had taken to be his bossiness and conceit, little knowing that it was only a front for the tender and sensitive person inside, who had been through so much suffering. Her face sobered. She could only guess at the traumas he had faced alone, and vowed that she would do all in her power to make up to him for the dark days of the past.

\* \* \*

Next morning Tim turned up unexpectedly, with such an animated look about him that Helen immediately wondered what was up. Usually placid and unhurried by nature, today her brother positively leapt up the steps and into the house before she could utter a word.

'Have I got news for you!' he announced, dropping into a bentwood chair at the pine table and propping his legs up on another. On his feet were leather hiking boots.

'Good, bad or indifferent?' Helen asked warily, perching on a corner of the table nearby and swinging one slim jeans-clad leg.

'Good. Definitely good. And it concerns you.' He fished in an inside pocket of his waxed jacket and pulled out a sheaf of papers which he slapped down on the table-top. 'I've been very busy on your behalf after the fiasco of the Cretan fern.'

Helen peered over his shoulder. 'What have you done? Who did you see? And did you know that two men were here the other day, inspecting the mine ruins up in my field?'

Tim held up a large hand to halt the flow of questions. 'Keep quiet for a minute, and I'll tell you everything.

'I went to see my boss after that planning officer had showed you that report with my name on it.' He pointed to a paper. 'This one. And he said that the council had specially asked to see it — and to see anything else regarding the site that we might have. Apparently he knew that it was a triple SI. You know — a Site Of Special Scientific Interest, which neither you nor I did.

'Anyway,' Tim shuffled the documents in front of him and pulled one out to show her. 'The discovery of the fern was what spurred them into taking action over a scheme that had been hatching for some time.' He looked up at her for a moment. 'Do you know that the council has started doing up the old mine engine-houses in other parts of the country, conserving them for the future?' he asked.

Helen nodded. 'Yes, I read it in the paper a while ago, and the two men who came here mentioned it as well.'

'Well, I spoke to some people,' he went on, 'who pulled a few strings, and the outcome is — ' he paused for effect ' — that they will seriously consider your site as a priority.'

Tim shifted in his chair and placed his feet on the floor as he swivelled to pick up another paper which he referred to.

'Mainly,' he explained, 'because of the importance of getting the fern under official protection, but also because some of the industrial relics are worth preserving in their own right. The engine-house where the pump would have brought water up from underground is too derelict to save, unfortunately. But you do know that there are dressing floors up there, all overgrown, don't you? And concrete buddles surviving undamaged, and wooden leats as well, apart from masses of other as yet unidentified stuff?'

Helen held up two hands to stem the flow. 'Whoa, Tim! I haven't the faintest idea what you're talking about,' she said. 'It's too technical for me. I've been a city girl for most of my adult life, remember.'

'Then it's time you took an interest in what you've got on your own property,' he said firmly, rising to pace up and down the room.

Helen smiled. He was obviously getting into lecturing mode.

He waved an arm and began. 'Tin 'dressing' was what they called the process of separating the ore from the waste. This is where the famous 'bal-maidens' came in. You have heard of *them*, I suppose?' he said, giving her a withering look.

'Oh, yes,' Helen replied. 'They wore big white bonnets and worked with heavy hammers smashing up the stones.'

'Good. Well, the leats were chutes to carry water for washing the finer stuff after the women had broken it up. And the buddles were full of water too — with revolving paddles to separate out the really fine stuff. Tin would sink to the bottom and impurities would float on top and be swept away. Got it?'

'Yes, sir, thank you, sir, you're a good

lecturer, sir,' Helen said, laughing.

'Oh, sorry,' Tim said, looking shame-faced. 'Was I getting carried away?'

'You were,' said Helen, 'but I'll forgive you. It was quite interesting really. And you're right — I'd better know at least something about what's on my doorstep.'

'Well, now for the good news.' Tim grinned at her. 'They're prepared to make you an offer for the land. They want to buy it from you. You'll receive official notification in a few days.'

'And you've waited all this time to tell me that? Jabbering away about tin processing when all the time you knew! Tim, that's fantastic!' she exclaimed. 'And I was so mad at you when I thought you . . . Oh, thank you, thank you so much!'

'Oh, it was nothing,' he replied with fake modesty. He gathered up the documents and stuffed them back into his pocket. 'And as a reward,' he glanced at his watch, 'I will stay to lunch, thanks. If you've got anything suitable for a genius to eat, that is.'

'Tim Matthews, you're impossible!' She gave him a mock cuff round the ear. 'But I don't know what I'd do without you.' And she slid down from the table to put the kettle on.

# A Good Omen

Helen was tidying the kitchen later on — or at least, she was trying to look as if she was. Her mind was in turmoil as she tried to come to terms with all that had happened in such a short space of time. Two such momentous changes — changes which were to affect her whole life — happening in quick succession like this, took a lot of getting used to.

She tossed aside the cloth with which she had been half-heartedly wiping down surfaces and leaned her elbows on the windowsill, gazing out across the back of her property until her eyes were drawn to the field.

She could go ahead now with her plans to expand her holiday lets by making the rest of the land into a campsite, which would be the culmination of all her hopes and dreams.

On the other hand, if she and Martin were to set up home together, where would that leave her with the business?

Which did she want most? She would have to choose, for she could hardly have both. Martin would naturally expect her to go and live in his new bungalow and help him to bring up Clare. What would he think when she told him about this turnaround in her fortunes?

Her head was reeling as her brain teemed with unanswerable questions.

She was jerked back to the present by a short ring at the door and a shout as Martin let himself in. She went to meet him and he folded her into his arms, burying his face in her hair.

'I had to pinch myself when I woke up this morning, to be sure that this is real,' he said as they walked into the lounge.

'Oh, it is,' Helen breathed, gazing at him with stars in her eyes. 'I've had so much to think about since yesterday, though, that I haven't really been able to take it all in yet. Martin, I have to tell you something.' She took a deep breath. 'Tim came round this morning. And he brought me some fantastic news.'

Haltingly she told him the whole story.

'So together with all that happened yesterday, I feel like I'm living in a dream world,' she finished. 'And I've got so much on my mind I can't think straight.' She turned to him with a serious expression. 'We have such a lot to talk about.'

'We certainly have. How about going for a walk?' he replied. 'I always find that I can think and talk better in the open air, don't you?'

Helen nodded. 'OK,' she replied, 'but tell me first where we're going, so I know which shoes to wear this time!'

Martin chuckled. 'How about St Agnes Beacon? Right to the top. That'll mean stout walking shoes. All right?' He was wearing sturdy trainers himself.

'Sounds OK to me,' she replied and went to rummage in the cupboard under the stairs where she kept her shoes.

The air was clear and balmy as they climbed the fairly gentle slope of the beacon, through clumps of heather and outcrops of rough granite bedrock. Larks sang high overhead, tiny almost invisible specks against a sky of cloudless blue.

Reaching the top of the hill, they flung themselves down on a carpet of springing heather to get their breath back.

'You see, Martin,' Helen began thoughtfully, as she plucked a long piece of grass and twisted it round in her fingers, 'this offer for the land has come just as I'd given up all hope of ever succeeding in my business. You know how much I've wanted to prove that I could do it — and prove it to myself as much as anyone.' She smiled up at him. 'Do you remember when we first met, when you came striding down the path as Jane and I were getting out of the car?'

His eyes twinkled. 'I'll say I do. I was thinking how attractive you were even then.'

'And I thought you were the most arrogant, pushy . . . ' Helen giggled. 'Which made me even more determined to make a go of the business, you see. Because you told me straight that I would never do it.'

'I underestimated you, my love.' He dropped a kiss on top of her head.

'But now, you see,' she said as she turned to meet his eyes, 'I don't know what we're going to do. How you feel about it . . . What our future plans will be . . . I'm in such a quandary that I can't settle to anything until I talk it all over with you. Do you understand what I mean?'

'Of course I understand. And I'm delighted that your problems have been solved. It's a marvellous solution and I've been trying to take it all in since you told me about it.'

'But — ' Helen interrupted.

'No, let me finish,' said Martin. 'I've

got a suggestion to make, so hear me out before you say anything.' He paused and looked down into her face. 'How about this: you go ahead, get the campsite up and running like you planned to do. And put in a manager to look after it from then on.'

Helen's eyes widened and she sat up. 'A manager?' she repeated blankly.

'Yes,' said Martin. 'Think about it. You would still be doing all the bookings and administrative stuff — running the whole show like you are now. You just wouldn't live on the premises. Makes sense, doesn't it?'

And it did. A slow grin began to spread across Helen's face. The more she thought about it, the more sense it made, and she realised that this way she could have both worlds after all.

'Oh, Martin, it does!' With a beaming face she threw her arms around his neck. 'Why on earth didn't I think of it myself? It's so simple. Oh, you are *clever*!'

'And arrogant, and what else was it?

Pushy . . . and . . . ?' He ducked as she aimed a pretended cuff at his head.

Helen drew away, her thoughts racing again, and there was a pause for a few moments while she sat gazing out over the sea, immersed in her own thoughts. She was so still that a small butterfly that had been hovering over a foxglove spire nearby came and settled on her foot.

'Come back to me, Helen,' said Martin softly at last. 'Where are you?'

She jumped and the butterfly took off, up and away, looking like a fragment of the sky itself.

'I was just wondering,' she said, 'whether Jane might possibly be interested in being manager. I'd need to have someone totally trustworthy and reliable, wouldn't I? And she does love it down here. That would be ideal, although it would be a lot to expect of her, wouldn't it — to change her entire lifestyle . . . ?'

'You won't know how she would feel until you've talked it over with her,'

Martin pointed out reasonably.

'What do you think about it, though?' she asked, pulling absent-mindedly at the grass by her side

'I think it's an excellent idea, but right now there's something more pressing that I want to ask you.'

His voice was full of meaning and she looked up sharply. He was looking straight at her and his eyes held a depth of softness she'd never seen before as he took her hands in his.

'Helen, my darling, I've loved you from the first time we met. I think I knew then that we were meant to be together, although it's been a tough ride since.'

Helen gasped and put a hand to her lips.

He smiled into her eyes and stroked the back of her hand with one finger as he finished softly, 'And knowing all about me and about Clare, too, would you consider — oh, my love, will you marry me?'

Helen slipped her arms around his

waist and laid her face against his warm neck, not even having to think about her answer.

'Of course I will,' she said with a contented sigh. For she knew now that she had always loved this man, though she hadn't allowed herself to admit it. Her true feelings had been over-shadowed by the surface anger and bitterness that had arisen through their misunderstandings.

Now she felt that she'd come home at last after a long, rough journey, and she never wanted to go away again.

A long time passed as they lay on the sweet-smelling turf and talked of plans for the future, of the many options which faced them, and of their past lives, opening their hearts and sharing their innermost secrets, each striving to learn all there was to know about the other.

And after that they didn't talk at all for a while, but lay wrapped in each other's arms while the sun moved slowly down the sky, turning the sea to beaten silver and streaking the small clouds with shades of powder pink and apricot.

\* \* \*

A few days later Martin called in unexpectedly towards early evening as Helen was sitting in the bay window of the lounge, relaxing with a cup of tea.

Her face lit up as she saw him coming and she ran out to meet him and raised her face for his kiss. Although they had spent long periods on the phone to each other, it was the first time they'd actually been together since the day Martin had proposed.

'Oh, it's so good to see you,' she said as they rocked for a moment in each other's arms. 'Come in and have a cup of tea, I've just made some.'

Swinging hands they went into the house. Martin was still in his business clothes, though he had discarded the jacket of his suit.

'I'm on my way back from work and came round to show you something,' he explained.

'Oh?' Helen, busy with the kettle, had her back to him and looked over her shoulder with interest. Martin had perched on a corner of the table and was swinging one leg as he reached into his trouser pocket and pulled out a small box.

'I wanted you to have this before now,' he said, 'but I've taken longer than I expected to find just the right thing. I hope you like it, sweetheart. If not, I can take it back and we can choose something else together. But I wanted to give you a surprise, you see.'

He watched anxiously as Helen snapped open the square velvet ring-box, and there on a white satin cushion lay a heavy gold band set with a magnificent diamond solitaire encircled with brilliants making it look like the petals of a daisy.

Helen gasped and tears sprang to her eyes as she touched it wonderingly.

'Oh, Martin, it's absolutely beautiful!' she whispered.

He visibly relaxed. 'It's antique. I really hoped you would like it — but I can change it if you'd rather have something else.'

'Of course not! I love it!' she said, lifting it out of the box.

He took it from her and placed it gently on her finger.

'How does it feel?' he asked.

'It's a perfect fit,' Helen replied, turning it to make sure. 'You clever thing — how did you know?'

'Guesswork.' He smiled. 'The young woman who served me had hands about the same size as yours, so I asked her to try it on.'

'Oh, thank you, thank you!' Helen reached for him and he swept her into his arms to seal their promise with a tender kiss.

When they eventually dragged themselves apart and were sitting at the table drinking their cooling tea, she said pensively, 'I don't suppose we can even think of setting a date for the wedding for ages. There's so much to do first.'

'Like getting two bungalows built, for a start.' Martin smiled. 'I'll get that work underway just as soon as the paperwork comes through. And you can contact Jane and send out a few feelers. Let her get used to the idea gradually. Didn't you say she's coming down for a holiday sometime?'

'Yes, but not until September, so I've got plenty of time to work on her,' she replied.

'So,' said Martin thoughtfully, 'I should say that we'll have to give it a year at the most, maybe a little less if things come together sooner. What do you think?'

Helen nodded. 'It seems such a long time to wait,' she said wistfully, holding her hand up to the light and admiring the shining stones. 'But I know how busy we'll be.'

'We certainly will — and that'll make the time fly, you'll see.' Martin stood up and picked up his mug of tea. 'Let's sit

outside and finish this. It's a lovely
evening and I've been cooped up
indoors all day.'

Helen followed him out through the
back door and they wandered up the
path as far as the hedge that bordered
the field, leaned on the gate and looked
over as they sipped their tea.

'I've been wondering,' she said as her
gaze fell on the Sphinx and the other
statues still lying where they had left
them. 'What am I going to do with
those? I had an idea once that I would
restore Aunt Grace's garden, but that's
no good now since the campsite will go
ahead after all.'

'Mm,' he said thoughtfully. 'That
collection ought to be kept together
really. I mean, there's all that bric-a-
brac you've got in those boxes in the
garage, and her photographs, as well as
these.' He waved a hand in the direction
of the statues. 'They deserve to be on
display somewhere.'

'Yes.' Helen said, thoughtfully as she
gazed up the field. Suddenly she turned

and clutched at his arm. '*I* know,' she said. 'I know just the thing! There's a museum in St Agnes, right?'

'Yes. It's only a little place though.' He looked doubtful.

'But the big things would go outside,' said Helen, warming to her theme. 'I'm sure they could find space for the smaller stuff. After all, people must be giving them things all the time. Where else do their exhibits come from?'

'Well, we can ask them, I suppose,' he returned with a shrug.

Helen looked into his face. 'I'd really like that,' she said. 'To keep Grace's things in her home town would be lovely. They might even agree to call it the 'Grace Tregonning Collection' or something, so that people will remember her. Mum would like that,' she added with a smile. 'But, Martin,' she went on slowly, 'not all of those photographs. Some of them are too personal. I'm talking about the ones of Grace and her camel driver, you know? I'd like to keep them myself.'

He nodded. 'I understand. There's no need for anyone else to come to the same conclusions as we did — whether we were right or not. It's an intriguing mystery and that's the way it shall stay.'

He dropped a kiss on the end of her nose and they returned to the house together.

★　★　★

On Sunday a few days later, Helen and Martin were once more up on the cliffs in their favourite sheltered nook, soaking up the sun.

Helen had been lying flat on her back with her arms behind her head when she suddenly noticed it. A bird of prey had come soaring in from the sea and was settling on an outcrop of rock nearby. With back and wings of slate grey and breast barred with white, its haughty profile was etched against the sky like a painting as it stared unblinkingly with one great shining eye at the intruders on its patch.

Helen nudged Martin and said, 'Look — a peregrine falcon. I've never seen one this close before. Isn't it beautiful?'

She willed the bird not to move as he shaded his eyes with a hand and followed her pointing finger.

'A falcon?' he said with awe. 'The emblem of Horus, the falcon-headed god, remember? He must have come to wish us luck.'

As he spoke, the bird spread its wings and took flight with effortless grace and sped straight towards the sun. Transfixed, they both watched it becoming smaller and smaller until it was swallowed up at last by the great golden rays of light and they could see it no longer.

'That has to have been an omen,' Helen whispered as she leaned into Martin's encircling arm.

A bank of purple cloud was now slowly enveloping the sun, which had become a fiery ball and was beginning to streak the sky with fingers of flame.

They were silent for a while, held

spellbound by the beauty of the place and still marvelling at the other-worldly visits of the peregrine, until Martin moved at last and brought them back to the present.

'That reminds me,' he said, as he fished in a pocket and brought out a crumpled leaflet.

'What's this?' she asked, and her eyes widened as Martin unfolded it and she saw that it was a page torn from a travel brochure. The illustration caught her eye immediately and her heart missed a beat. The Sphinx. And the great pyramids of Giza!

She raised excited eyes to his face. 'Wh-what . . . ?' she whispered.

'I thought a cruise down the Nile — if you'd like to. For our honeymoon,' he said gently.

But before she could reply, his mouth came down to cover hers, and Helen gave herself up to the sheer wonder of the moment and blissful dreams of the life which lay ahead for them both . . .